"Without science, … ssel," he bellowed. … have these electric lights."

He reached up and … ging, sending alternating band … faces that were gaping at his performance. Muir lifted his whiskey tumbler.

"And without science, you would not even have the glass to hold this dishwater you have the nerve to call whiskey."

He threw the glass against the wall. I winced, anticipating the shatter. It didn't come. The tumbler hit the wall…and kept going, disappearing from view and leaving a series of ripples behind in the solid steel, ripples that almost immediately hardened in place. The room fell silent save from a muttered "Bleeding hell" from the far side of the table. But no one was in the mood for laughing now.

"Is this it? Is it working?" the purser asked.

"It seems something is," Muir replied deadpan. "Maybe we should send a scientist to check?"

The Dunfield Terror

WILLIAM MEIKLE

Macabre Ink

ISBN 978-1-63789-624-2
Macabre Ink is an imprint of Crossroad Press Publishing

For information address Crossroad Press at 141 Brayden Dr., Hertford, NC 27944
www.crossroadpress.com

Cover art by Zach McCain

First Crossroad Press Edition - 2023

This one is dedicated to everyone who works through winter storms to make sure the rest of us can sleep easily.

ACKNOWLEDGEMENTS

And special thanks to Jim McLeod, whose Ginger Nuts of Horror blog is the best wee horror blog on the planet, and one that has done a lot for my profile in the business. Ta, Jimbo.

1

Present Day

I like riding the plow, especially when the wind howls like a banshee and snow spatters like gunshot against the window. I look after the fifteen-kilometer stretch of highway from Trinity heading south to Irving Station and on stormy nights I have it all to myself—it's just my hunk of mobile metal and me against the elements.

Round about these parts, there are plenty of elements to contend with. Most of the year round it's wind—lots of wind, and rain, heavy at times, torrential at others, in spring and autumn—if we ever get either. Some years there's just two seasons—winter and summer. And then there's February—a special case of hell hereabouts—a frozen hard month during which it's mostly blowing a gale and snowing. And that's on the good days. This wasn't one of those.

The storm had started that morning—flurries only at first, but with enough wind behind it to show its intent. It ramped up through mid-afternoon until it was dumping a couple of inches an hour in a raging gale. I'd been out in it with the plow since four o' clock—three hours straight now trying to keep at least a lane of the highway clear. I moved snow and once my back was turned the wind moved it back. Then we did it all again. Some nights I manage to keep the road clear until the storm blows out, on others I'm forced back to the depot to sulk. So far, we could just about call this one a draw, although I was starting to think I was going to lose.

I turned at the westernmost point of my route, in the gas station parking area. The station itself was quiet—the lights were on but there was no sign of any customers. Mary was moving about inside—I could just see her through the swirling snow. I debated stopping for coffee, a donut and a chat—Mary was always good company on nights like this, and she'd also like having a friendly face turn up, but the snow was coming down hard, and even ten minutes at this stage could mean big banks of drifts.

I headed back north, looking forward to an eventual break and that long-awaited coffee, although George and Jimmy would be poor substitutes for Mary's charms. I was thinking about her as the plow roared and did its thing, leaving a neat line of banked snow in my wake. I took the switchback at forty, singing along at the top of my voice to the music in my headphones.

I'm walking on sunshine.

I've been doing this most of my adult life—well, the winter parts at least. Some of the guys in the bar have told me that they don't know how I do it, night after night in the wind and cold and snow—but in truth, I find it kind of peaceful. And more than that—and here's something I don't tell those guys over a beer—for me, it's a duty, a way to pay my dues to the town that raised me. There's a kid along Witlow Road that thinks I'm a superhero, a dark avenger keeping the storm from engulfing his house. I kinda like that idea—secretly, of course—to admit it, especially among the beer crew, would lead to months of piss taking that would be well deserved.

It's not like I ever have any archenemies to deal with anyway. Once the storm really gets going, there's just the road and me—sometimes I'll see a moose or a coyote. Even rarer there'll be a car or pickup, following along gingerly in my wake, someone smart enough not to try to overtake the plow, but not quite smart enough to stay off the road on a night like this one.

Tonight was a quiet one. I had the run of the road to myself. All I saw was the almost mesmerizing dance of falling snow in the stretch lit by my lights, and the reflectors on the poles on the roadside to keep me on the straight and narrow. The snow was getting heavier still as I reached the high point of the switchback but that didn't bother me—I'd done this so often now I could do it in my sleep—indeed I often did, my winter dreams being full of dark road and white snow.

I was relaxed, so much in control that I almost didn't notice when things started to get weird.

It happened on the last dip of the switchback. Something caught my eye ahead, just off the left edge of the road, a lighter area in the darkness. At first it was just a patch of fog. It took me a few seconds to spot that it seemed to glow where it was picked up in the headlights. It appeared to be moving at speed, keeping the same distance between us as we climbed and crested the last hill before making our way down to Trinity Junction and sea level.

I tore off the headphones as my heart kicked into overdrive. I pushed the accelerator as hard as I dared, hoping against hope that the strange fog wasn't what I suspected it to be.

It matched my speed change—the glowing patch was doing fifty and accelerating as we descended, and it was still there just ahead and to the left when we reached the foot of the hill. I hit a slightly larger drift on the bend at the bottom as I tried to cut right and take the corner onto the Trinity road. The plow shuddered, sending a jolt up my spine that distracted me, took my attention off the road—just for a second, but it was as if the fog had been waiting for an opening. As I turned off the highway, it pounced—that's what it felt like—an animal on the attack. It swallowed the plow in a second. All of a sudden, I could see nothing out the windshield but opaque white. I was forced to slow down—I wasn't about to come to a halt though, so I kept the plow in as straight a line as I could manage and prayed.

Metal squealed, and the steering wheel bucked in my hand, threatening to drag the plow to the left. I knew enough to know there was a deep roadside ditch on that side, and just past that a steep fall off down to the inner bay. If I went down there, I might not be coming out until spring. I pulled hard to the right and got her straightened up, but something wasn't finished with me yet. The strange diffuse light still filled my view, and once again I heard metal squeal as if in tortured pain. A crack, loud like a gunshot in the plow's cabin, ran all the way up the window on my left door, and when I put my hand on it, the fingertips of my gloves started to smolder as if burning.

The pale glow outside got brighter.

I threw the plow right—not too far, as I also knew there was a smaller ditch on that side of the road. I went left again, ramming the accelerator to the floor—I was now extremely worried about something catching me than I was about not being able to see. Metal tore beneath the cab, and I had a bad moment when I feared I was caught up on a fallen branch but, with a screech that sounded like frustrated rage, the plow finally kicked in and I sped off and away along the narrow road. The pale glow faded; I could see the road again. The glowing fog receded in my rearview mirror and I remembered to breathe.

I knew immediately that I wasn't going to get much more work out of the big plow that night. The engine started to cough and splutter as I turned off the Bonaventure junction and into the campsite hollow, and something ground noisily on the road beneath me as I got into the town itself.

I managed to baby her along to the depot and arrived just as George Hislop was bringing in the heavy gritting truck from his turn around the town roads. I gave him a wave as I got out of the cab, but he wasn't paying any attention to me—he stared, wide-eyed, at the front of my rig. I closed my side door—new crack on the window and all—and walked round the front to get a look for myself.

"I think I hit something hard," I shouted.

George didn't reply. He was still looking at the blade of the plow—or rather, at what had been a blade until a few minutes ago. Now it was only a lump of twisted metal that looked like it had been melted then rapidly cooled into something that almost resembled its previous shape but was too twisted to ever work properly as a plow again. It certainly wouldn't be much further use to the town that winter.

I didn't even have to ask what could have done this—I knew only too well. I'd seen its work before.

George looked over at me.

"The fucker is back again—isn't it?"

"Yep—and this time it has come all the way up to the highway—have you heard of it doing that before?"

George had gone back to looking at the plow blade.

"Nope—never heard of it going much past the peninsula. But who knows with the fucker. This is going to be bad, isn't it?"

I nodded and headed inside the depot.

I had some calls to make.

2

From the journal of Duncan Campbell, March 1954

I need to get this down while it is yet fresh in my mind, and maybe the simple act of writing it will bring some focus and rational thought to the madness that has befallen our little experiment. I fear that what I have seen—and done—here will haunt me for many years to come, and I can only hope that this record may go in some small way toward convincing the powers that be to leave well enough alone. Despite our good intentions at the outset, it is now quite clear we should never have even entertained the thought in the first place, and I wish to blazes that I'd stayed at home when given the chance.

The military chaps are all over the story like a rash, of course—anything with the potential for destruction like we saw could not help but interest them. Muir has told them that nothing is salvageable, that the experiment was a total failure. But I know how their minds work. They will not be able to ignore it. They will want to poke and prod and examine and, ultimately, use it as a weapon.

It cannot be allowed.

"Get it done, or don't bother coming back."

That's what they said at the ministry just before they packed us off to Southampton to catch the naval vessel to Newfoundland. They told us it was for Queen and Country—a matter that might make the Empire great again—

groundbreaking was a word used more than once. What they didn't tell us was that the Atlantic crossing would be foul, the food would be worse, and the weather once we got to our destination would be subarctic, and getting colder by the day. What with that, and the suspicion shown to our small group of scientists by the enlisted men of the crew, it was not the happiest of boat trips, especially for someone like me, whose previous seagoing experience was limited to several trips on the Firth of Clyde ferries.

I stood on deck, a gale-force wind trying to blow me back to Blighty while simultaneously soaking me with spray. It was my turn to watch as a small group of frozen scientists and completely disgruntled sailors tried to put together Muir's patchwork contraption of chrome, wire and electrical components, all of which were a complete mystery to me. We'd been at anchor for an hour and I was already wishing I'd stayed home.

At least before the war they'd been sending me to warm, dry factories in the West Country to experiment on docile sheep and cattle unlikely to do me a mischief. But the Nazis changed everything; Hitler's thirst for a technological advantage meant that the Germans threw vast amounts of money into research—not just weapons but advanced biology and physics. They might have been mad bastards, but they advanced German science by leaps and bounds. And it wasn't until the fighting was over and the dust settled that we in Britain realized we were no longer rich enough to keep up.

That's when I got recruited to the think tank. I had a request to pop up to London, where I was ushered into a roomful of people I knew only by reputation. We had tea and scones with the minister, and, in return for a nice raise and the promise of a better pension, a simple directive.

"Come up with smart stuff nobody else has thought of yet."

Not much of a brief, but it had been enough for us to be going on with. Since the late forties, we'd got by with the occasional report, a couple of not-too-disastrous demonstrations, and the promise of results at an unspecified later date. It had been an easy, if uneventful, life, and I was already looking forward to early retirement, that promised pension, and some gentle rounds of golf.

Everything changed with the new decade. A new broom swept Whitehall, one that demanded results and almost brushed us away with the rest of the dross. Professor Muir arrived at the opportune moment and became both savior and Satan. He had a reputation to maintain—iconoclastic, eccentric and abrasive, but also undoubtedly brilliant. He'd been the man responsible for jamming the buzz bombs' guidance systems, for finding an antidote to a plague the populace never even got to hear of, and for finding a way to clog enemy harbors with rampant seaweed. I'd met him twice, at conferences in Edinburgh, and he always struck me as being ferociously intelligent—and knowing it. In another country he might be feted and honored with awards and medals—but in Britain he'd insulted too many people in power, rode roughshod over too many regulations. They gave him the think tank in the hope that he'd run us quickly into either oblivion or ignominy.

Instead, Muir once again did something remarkable.

My own specialty is in mammalian biology, with chemistry second and applied mathematics a distant—very distant—third. Muir's explanation that we sat through back at the ministry had gone completely over my head. The only bit I understood was his opening, and closing, questions.

What if we could make a battleship invisible?

The professor had made some esoteric calculations on many sheaves of paper, and had brought along a small contraption of chrome, copper and wire that he invited us all to inspect before making the minister's fountain pen disappear. He couldn't bring it back again of course, and there were many around that table that accused him of sleight of hand and trickery, but Muir had done just enough to persuade the ministry that a field trial was at least a possibility. They in turn insisted on somewhere away from prying eyes. With the help of our friends, the Canadians, we started to plan the trip to Newfoundland, although I will admit that I did canvass hard for an alternative spot in a quiet bay in the Mediterranean.

But Newfoundland in what passed for spring in these parts it was to be, and after several months of frantic preparation, Muir finally announced he was ready. I still had little clue as to how he proposed to do it, or even whether it was at all possible, for the final experiments had been undertaken above my clearance level. For a while I even held out hope that Muir meant to take the trip without me altogether, but that was dashed three days before departure.

"I need you, Duncan," he said, mollifying me somewhat with a large glass of some excellent Scotch. "You keep me on the ground. Besides, a trip like this can never have enough Scotsmen."

We both laughed at that, but there was something in my countryman's eyes I hadn't seen before. It looked like doubt—and possibly more than a trace of fear. Whatever it was, he wouldn't be drawn on the matter, even after we'd made serious inroads into the whiskey. All I got from him was a muttered oath.

"Damned stupid research assistants who cannot follow simple instructions deserve all that they get. It is not my fault if they can't get themselves out of a spot of bother."

In the morning I had a stinker of a hangover, but I remembered what Muir had said. I asked around. Dick Roberts, a young lab technician, hadn't been seen for several days, but that was all that was known, all anybody knew. I didn't get to the truth of the matter until much later—and by then, of course, it was far too late.

Young Roberts was only the first of many.

I was thinking about Muir's bottle of Scotch while I stood on the windy deck of the battleship. A dram or two would have been most welcome at that point, but I knew better than to leave my post. I might not be a naval man, but on this trip, it was best to obey the chain of command; it was either that or risk a stint in the brig. Captain Squire had taken pains early on to show that he was in charge and would not hesitate to prove it. At some point I knew that he and Muir would have a serious disagreement, but so far, they had kept to their separate corners. I only hoped the peace lasted long enough to get the job done.

I was brought out of my reverie by a shout from Muir himself.

"Let them know we're ready," he called out. It was finally time for my one bit of action in the proceedings. I made the signal to the watchers on the shore some four hundred yards away. Even from here I could see that their tent on the exposed promontory was billowing and blowing in the increasing gale, but I saw their answer clear enough. They too were ready.

I gave Muir the nod, and did the same again in Captain Squire's direction to show that I acknowledged his authority. Muir was not so polite. He stepped forward and, without further ado, threw a lever on his box of tricks.

Nothing of any consequence happened. Something sparked, and there was a distinct hum that lasted for maybe three seconds. All I could hear was more wind, and all I felt was cold spray in my face. I turned away in time to see Captain

Squire's smirk before he headed for the relative warmth to be had inside. I lingered just long enough to have a word with the professor.

Muir did not seem too perturbed by the outcome.

"A blown valve," he said. "I forgot to factor in the effect of the degaussing panels. These things happen. Give me an hour and we'll try again."

But the hour turned into two, then three, and Muir's temper frayed with the dimming of the light. By the time it came round to sunset, he had to give up hope of getting anything done that day.

"It's the blasted spray and drizzle," he said as we made our way to the captain's quarters for pre-dinner drinks. "It's causing too many shorts."

Squire heard that as we entered.

"Perhaps some kind of umbrella might be in order?" he said, and laughed long and loud, which only caused Muir's brows to furrow deeper and his mood to darken further. When we finally got round to eating, it was obvious an explosion was imminent.

Mr. Jones, the purser, tried to lighten the mood by telling a long, involved tale of shore leave, a brothel, and a Spanish prostitute who was more man than many of the sailors, but it fell mostly on deaf ears. The captain seemed determined to rub Muir's nose in what he deemed already to be a failure.

"You do know that the Yanks tried this already?" Squire said, loud enough for all to hear. "Back in '43, with the *Etheridge*, I believe. A bloody disaster all around, or so I'm told. At least you've managed to avoid that."

At first Muir tried to control himself.

"I am well aware of the research, and the reasons for that debacle, thank you very much. I am not about to recreate that mistake," he said. "I have carefully modulated all of the substream harmonics and ensured that the frequency shifts are calibrated. I…"

Squire interrupted him again by laughing loudly.

"There's your typical scientist, gentlemen. Never uses one big word when two will do. It's no wonder that everything they touch turns to ashes and dust."

"And there's your typical military man, gentlemen," Muir replied, so loud that everyone else fell silent. "So full of his own self-importance and narrow-minded regimentation that he cannot recognize the worthiness of anything but his own kind."

The professor started warming to his topic. I put a hand on his arm, hoping to mollify him somewhat, but he was too deep in his anger for that.

"Without science, you would not have this fine vessel," he bellowed. "Without science you would not have these electric lights." He reached up and set the overhead lamp swinging, sending alternating bands of shadow and light over all the faces that were gaping at his performance. Muir lifted his whiskey tumbler. "And without science, you would not even have the glass to hold this dishwater you have the nerve to call whiskey."

He threw the glass against the wall. I winced, anticipating the shatter. It didn't come. The tumbler hit the wall…and kept going, disappearing from view and leaving a series of ripples behind in the solid steel, ripples that almost immediately hardened in place.

The room fell silent save from a muttered *"Bleeding hell"* from the far side of the table. But no one was in the mood for laughing now.

"Is this it? Is it working?" the purser asked.

"It seems something is," Muir replied deadpan. "Maybe we should send a scientist to check?"

We made our way swiftly up on deck to find that the ship was becalmed in dense fog, gathered around us so thickly that I could only just make out the bow to my left and the gun turrets to my right although they were mere yards away. The fog had a distinctly eerie quality, almost a glow that I put down at the time to it picking up and dispersing reflections from the lights strung on deck.

Muir wasted no time examining the weather conditions. He headed toward the experiment. He hadn't quite reached it when the first scream pierced the night. I turned toward the sound, and was just in time to see a sailor sink into the deck, as if he'd fallen into a pool of water. He waved his arms, and what had been metal *splashed*, slowly, as if thick and viscous, sending ripples across several yards of deck. The man opened his mouth to scream again. The liquid flowed and spilled down his gullet. Then, as quickly as it had liquefied, it hardened, and became solid metal once more.

The sailor was mercifully quite dead by the time I reached him, trapped at the neck as if buried upright in the deck, the lower part of his face obscured by a metal mask and his eyes, still horrorstruck, staring straight at me.

"Turn that bloody thing off before anyone else gets hurt," I shouted. Muir didn't move. I left the stricken sailor, strode across the deck and grabbed the professor's arm, turning him around until we stood nose to nose. "Turn it off," I yelled into his face.

He replied, remarkably calmly.

"That's going to prove to be somewhat difficult, Duncan. It isn't switched on."

I wheeled away from him and looked for myself. I saw immediately that he had told the truth; the contraption of wires, valves and coils sat in the middle of the deck, inert and silent.

"So, what the blazes is happening?"

Muir shook his head.

"I don't rightly know. Maybe some residual effect from when we started it up earlier; maybe something got started that would have been stopped if we kept going. Maybe…"

"There's a few too many maybes there for my liking," I replied.

He nodded.

"Mine too. But I need more information before I can hypothesize."

A shot rang out from the stern, bringing all speculation to an abrupt end as more screams filled the sudden silence that followed.

When I reached the stern, I was at first unsure exactly what was happening, for the fog was, if anything, even thicker here…so thick that it looked almost solid. That thought proved rather too close to reality as a waft of wind blew a denser area over the top of three sailors nearby. They reacted as if hit by a wall of searing flame. Flesh melted and sloughed off their bones in oily sheets even as their screams tore at my ears. Mercifully it was all over almost before I had time to move. Another breeze wafted past, the denser fog moved away to starboard, and we were left on a quiet deck with only the brutalized bodies to remind us of what had just happened.

Captain Squire had momentarily lost his air of command, and looked more like a startled accountant than a naval officer; he stood, rooted to the spot, staring at the bloody smears that were all that was left of the crewmen. I had to manhandle him away forcibly, and when he finally decided to move, he did so with the blank, almost lifeless, stare of a man in deep shock.

Muir reacted to the situation the fastest of us all.

"Get below. Get below now. It could happen again at any moment."

As one we headed for the hatchway.

We didn't all make it.

We got close to the main storm door leading below, just as thicker fog wafted over the bulwarks. Metal warped, buckled and melted. A young lieutenant—to this day I have never even learned his name—leapt between us and the fast-approaching fog.

"Get the captain below," he yelled.

And those were his last words. The fog fell on him, and once again the result was the same as before. Muir didn't let me wait to see the man's final end. He dragged the captain to the doorway, I jumped in after them, and the professor heaved the storm door shut behind us with an almighty *clang*. The metal warped, rippled, then hardened again with a series of creaks and moans that sounded almost human.

Everything fell silent.

The fog had moved off again.

I remembered to breathe. We were still alive.

But for how long?

It took a lot of shouting, ordering and threats of a spell in the brig, but eventually the remaining officers got the crew together in the main mess room. As a man, they looked to the captain, expecting orders, reassurance…leadership. I saw in their eyes the fear that threatened to grip me so tight I could no longer function. All of us eyed the walls and ceiling, ready for flight at the slightest hint of *softness*. We jumped at even the quietest of sounds and tried not to think of what the fog might do to us if we were caught in it.

The captain was in no better state than the rest of us, but Muir, who seemed made of sterner stuff, took charge of that matter at least. He went to the officer's quarters and returned with three fingers of Scotch in a tumbler, refusing to let the captain abstain from drinking it.

"Get it inside you, man," he said. "There's a reason it's called the *water of life*."

Twin spots of color appeared at the captain's cheeks as the liquor hit his stomach and went to work. His eyes cleared and he looked at Muir as if seeing him for the first time.

"What the blazes have you done, man?" he whispered.

"I don't know. Yet," Muir replied. "But leave that part to me. You need to get control of this ship. Your crew need you."

That simple call to duty was what the captain needed. He stood up straight, his training and experience took over, and he stepped up onto a table to address the men. Muir pulled me aside for a confab, so I missed Squire's speech, but even from the far corner of the galley I saw that he had the men's attention, and the fear had receded somewhat from their eyes.

We might get out of this yet.

"I hope you have a plan, old man," I said to Muir. "For I'm afraid I haven't a clue."

Muir looked grim.

"Somehow, we've managed to alter the very fabric of space," he said. "And I'm not sure there is anything that can be done about it."

"You'd best get your thinking cap on then," I replied. "I don't intend to just hang around to be melted like a wax candle."

My statement was amplified by a shout from one of the crew. It was addressed to the captain.

"We should take to the lifeboats. Right now."

Both Muir and I saw that the captain was considering the option. Muir strode over and stood below the officer looking up.

"It's not safe," he said.

Squire laughed bitterly.

"Where is?"

Muir had no answer to that one, but he still had his bluster.

"We have no idea as to the extent of this fog. At least in here we have some kind of protection that the lifeboats would not afford us. The metal in the hull seems sufficient to hold it at bay."

"And what exactly is *it*?" Jones the purser said, loud enough for all to hear.

Everyone fell silent. That was the single question we all needed to be answered. Muir's reply echoed what he had told me seconds before.

"It's some kind of flux in the fabric of space. We may have inadvertently caused a tear, allowing something from beyond, or between, to slip through to this plane of existence."

"Dinnae talk pish, man," a heavily accented Scots sailor shouted, and that got a nervous laugh from around the room.

"I ain't never heard of a place where they've got fog that bloody eats people," a Cockney voice chimed in.

"Maybe we're in Hell?" another answered, and as quickly as that they were all talking and shouting above each other. The meeting threatened to descend into chaos until Squire bellowed at the top of his voice.

"That's quite enough of that nonsense," he shouted. "This is still a ship of Her Majesty's Navy. Let's act like it."

Muir stepped up onto the table alongside the captain.

"We just need to keep calm," he said. "There's a scientific explanation for this, I'm sure of it."

"Aye?" the Scotsman who'd spoken before shouted back. "Well, you can take your scientific explanation, and shove it up your scientific arse."

Another round of laughter ran around the room, but I didn't join in. Something had caught my attention; at first I thought it was caused by a nervous tic in the corner of my eye, but it was more than that.

Much more.

One of the large extractor units in the ceiling above the main stoves was melting, running like hot wax.

The phenomenon, whatever it was, wasn't just back. It had penetrated the hull and was inside with us.

I tried had to remain calm as I walked forward to stand beneath Muir. I kept my voice low, hoping only he and maybe the captain, would hear.

"We've got trouble," I said. "It's got inside."

Muir nodded and forced a smile, as if I'd just told him a joke. He looked out over the crew.

"Given that the hull seems to be providing us some degree of protection, I suggest we put as much metal as possible between us and the outside? Somewhere farther below deck perhaps?"

The captain nodded.

"We shall make for the engine room," he said. "And give the professor here time to think our way out of this."

"Bugger that for a lark," the Scots sailor shouted. "I'll no' be cooped up like a rat in a trap. I'm headed for a lifeboat. And if you want to stop me, you'll have to shoot me."

"That can be arranged," the captain said coolly, and when I looked round at him, he had a pistol in his hand, aiming straight at the Scot. "Mutiny is a hanging offense, but we're short of a rope right now so this will have to do."

The big Scot looked around, looking for support from his shipmates.

"We can rush him. He can't shoot us all."

But no one seemed keen to attempt it. Besides, I saw that the *melting* area was growing fast, encroaching farther into the room.

"Captain," I said. "We have to go. Now."

He nodded, but never took his eyes off the big Scot.

"Get to the engine room, on the double," he barked. "We'll deal with your insubordination once we're all safe."

Squire turned and pointed to the door.

"Civilians first," he said, and waved the pistol in such a manner that we knew better than to argue. Muir and I headed to the doorway. We had just reached it when there was an almighty commotion behind us in the mess.

We'd left our retreat too late.

The fog had found its way fully inside, and the crew had now seen it. A melee immediately formed as too many men tried to cram through the narrow door. Muir, the purser, Squire and myself were the only ones that had made it out before the scrum.

"I will have order," Squire shouted, but fear held the crew in its grip. That, and the sound of screams rising from inside the galley caused the frantic mob to get even more agitated.

A single scream rang out, so anguished and forlorn that it stunned everyone else into silence for a moment, before the scrambling resumed with even greater intensity. Punches were thrown that would floor an ox, eyes were gouged, heads were stamped on and hair was pulled from its roots as men climbed over their friends and crew mates to try to reach safety. And all the time the screams grew wilder and more piteous behind them.

Men started to make their way out into the corridor, the press of bodies finally forcing us to back away to avoid being crushed ourselves. The metal in the doorway from which the crew was making their escape began to melt and buckle.

"Fall back," Squire shouted. "We'll regroup in the engine room."

It was obvious there was no alternative. We made off at speed down the corridor.

The screams of the dying followed us all the way.

We did not make it to the engine room. In fact, we only made it ten yards before Muir stopped dead in his tracks ahead of me. I almost ran him over, and Jones the purser barreled into me too before we all came to a stumbling halt. I immediately saw why the professor had acted. The whole corridor ahead of us seemed vague and unformed; the walls themselves were only a little more substantial than smoke. The floor rippled and swelled, as if pulled and pushed by tidal forces, the wavelets reaching almost to our toes.

I stepped back, hoping to move out of reach, but felt the weight and press of bodies at our rear.

"Stay back," Muir shouted.

"You don't get to tell me what to do," a voice I recognized replied, and the loud Scots sailor pushed his way past me. I tried to hold him back, but he shrugged me off easily.

"Come on, lads, let's take to the boats."

He took another step, his foot hit the deck… and kept on going. The big man lost his balance and fell forward, floundering. He shouted an oath, flapped his arms, then he was just *gone*, swallowed up as the deck rippled, then calmed. The metal pinged and creaked as it hardened once more. Something lay at my feet. I bent, and almost retched at the sight. It was a thumb, callused and tough...and neatly severed at the base, as if sliced by the keenest of blades. A dribble of blood ran from it. It was all that was left to show that the Scot had ever been there.

I'm afraid to say that I almost lost my composure, gripped by the certainty that we were all mere seconds from the same doom. If Muir hadn't taken matters in hand, I might have just sat down and waited for my fate. Before I could do anything, he took a step forward. I held my breath as his foot touched the deck. Muir planted his foot firmly, putting his weight on it. The deck held. The sense of mist and vagueness in the corridor had passed again.

For now.

"Quickly," Muir said. "I'm starting to get an idea of what's going on here."

We followed him down the corridor. Then, instead of heading down toward the engine room, he made for the storm door that led back out onto deck. He tried to push it open, but the previous damage done to it meant it was badly warped in its fitting. It creaked under his efforts, but did not give.

"Lend me a hand here, Duncan," the professor said.

"Wouldn't we be safer below?"

He shook his head.

"I'm coming to believe we are not safe anywhere. Now push."

I did as I was bid, and between us we forced the door open. The screech of metal on metal was almost deafening. Then again, so was the silence that fell as we got the door fully opened and looked outside.

The whole length of the deck looked like a candle that had been left in bright sunlight, having gone slightly soft, then hardened again. The metal rose and fell in hard ripples, as if a wave had washed over it then gone firm.

"Look, Duncan. Do you see?" Muir whispered at my ear.

At first all I could see was fog, curling and roiling everywhere. I had no wish to step out into it.

"Do you see?" Muir asked, more insistent this time. "It hasn't been affected at all."

He was speaking about the coils and chrome of the experiment. The machinery still sat on a seemingly unaffected part of deck, and there was no sign that any of it had been melted or malformed in any way.

"Get the crew over there," Muir said to Squire. "Get everybody in a circle around it. It may be our only hope."

If the captain took any slight from being given what amounted to an order, he didn't have time to complain. A wail of terror from back in the corridor was the signal of another appearance of the phenomenon. I could not see through the throng of bodies, but the sound froze the blood in my veins, and the memory of that severed thumb reminded me only too well of what must be happening.

Muir didn't wait. He stepped out onto the deck.

"Come on, Duncan. We must take the chance. It may be our only hope."

A fresh scream from the corridor convinced me. I followed Muir out the door, expecting at any second for my foot to disappear into melted metal, or for a thicker fog to fall on me and start to burn. But for those few seconds it took to cross the deck, luck was finally on our side and we reached the experiment with no further mishap. I helped Squire and the purser arrange the crew around the contraption, and was dismayed to see that less than half of the men who had gathered in the mess room had made it out to the relative safety of where we now stood.

"Maybe they have found another route," Jones the purser said, hopefully, but I saw the look that passed between Squire and Muir.

Those of us who had made it out on to the deck were the only survivors.

The fog swirled and rolled thickly around us, and we drew back into a tighter circle around Muir's contraption. The deck beyond the circle buckled, flowed and hardened where the fog passed. But none of us were in the least affected, and I started to hope that the worst might be over, that Muir had indeed found a way to keep us safe, for a time, at least.

I even relaxed enough to remember the pack of cigarettes in my pocket, and for a few seconds I was the most popular man on deck as I passed smokes around. Normally Muir would have joined me, but he was now completely intent on the contraption. I went over and stood at his side.

"What's the plan?" I asked.

He didn't reply at first, then took my smoke from me, took a lungful and handed it back.

"I'm considering our next move," he said. "We might have to switch it on again."

I hadn't heard Squire approach, but when he spoke, he was at my shoulder.

"After what it's done already? I can't allow that."

"We may not have a choice in the matter," Muir said. "Or do you intend to stand here for eternity, waiting for conditions to change in our favor?"

"This fog will clear," Squire said. "Fog always does, eventually."

"Not this one," Muir said softly. "I have been considering its behavior. The phenomena associated with it have been appearing in a loose spiral pattern…and we are currently at the center of that spiral."

I mapped out the ship and the deaths so far in my mind. Muir was right in his thinking, but I didn't see how it helped. He, however, had thought it through more than I had.

"I believe I might be able to predict where the soft spots occur; and I also believe that if I switch this machine on, we can effectively freeze the fog in place around us, allowing us a clear passage to the lifeboats."

I saw hope grow in the captain's face.

"I thought the boats were a bad idea?" he said.

Muir looked grim.

"And well they might be. But I for one will not stand around here just waiting to die."

Squire laughed with little humor.

"We may make a naval man out of you yet, Professor. Do what needs to be done. I'll prepare the men."

I spent the next twenty minutes alternately watching Muir fiddle with wiring and dials and eyeing the swirling fog, trying to ascertain any pattern in its movements. Squire had passed orders to be ready to make for the boats on his order. The crewmen around us grew increasingly restless, especially as the deck just outside our protected circle was now contorted and buckled into a nightmare landscape of peaks and troughs, spires and deep dark holes.

"Nearly done," Muir said when I asked. At almost the same instant, the deck bucked beneath us. Two crewmen fell, off-balance, and tumbled away from the protected area. The fog fell on them as if it was a predator that had been waiting for the opportune moment to strike, and once again we were forced to watch as death melted through the sailors.

"It has penetrated the hull below water level," Squire said. "Whatever you're going to do, best do it now. We're sinking."

"On my mark, run," Muir said. He reached for a lever and pulled it down. The air filled with a resonant hum. The fog swirled up and away from where it had descended on the two men and danced around where we stood.

"It's working," Squire shouted.

Muir still looked grim. "Well, it's doing something at least." He turned a dial. The hum grew to a drone and raised in pitch, ever higher, to a high whine that grated at the ears. The fog stopped swirling and hung, like a blanket, just above our heads.

"Run," Muir shouted.

None of us needed a second telling. We ran, picking our way through the ruin of the deck, trying to not look at the fog just above us.

The whine from Muir's contraption went up another notch, pressure bringing a sharp ache in my ears. The deck bucked beneath us again and the ship listed sharply to starboard. One man fell into a hole and went, screaming, down into a black deep that soon went silent. Another tumbled head-first into a metal spire that impaled him through the chest, stopping his heart in an instant.

The rest of us didn't stop. We rushed headlong for the port side, hoping against hope that the boats there were still seaworthy. The deck was now at such a slope that it became almost a matter of climbing to reach the hanging lifeboats, but it was with enormous relief that we found two boats still there, showing no signs of having been affected by the ravages of the fog. We clambered into them as best as we were able; luckily there was no repeat of the scrum that had occurred in the mess room.

Muir and Squire were last aboard. Squire gave the order, and my stomach leapt to my throat as we fell through mist to land with a bone-crashing splash in the sea.

We had only just righted ourselves when the ship above us listed sharply again, the prow rising as the rear sank. The whine from Muir's contraption cut off, as if someone had pulled a plug. The static fog once again started to seethe and roil in the air above the sinking vessel. And it was now spreading, sending out tendrils across the deck…and down the sides of the hull.

"Row, you buggers," Muir shouted. "Row like your lives depend on it."

The crew took to the oars. The other boat got the message, and they too began to row, but the short delay cost them dearly. A thicker patch of fog fell on the rear end of their boat even as they turned and began to move away. I closed my eyes, unwilling to see what was impossible to prevent. Seconds later, the screaming started, but it was mercifully short. When I opened my eyes, there was nothing to see but debris in the water…and a tendril of fog, almost luminescent, stretching ever closer to our own lifeboat.

The rowers could see it all too clearly. Our doom was coming straight for us. Beyond that, the ship was sinking fast, the prow raised high in the air, the fog curling and writhing, buckling the hull and tearing the vessel apart even as it went under, hissing and groaning like a dying beast.

"Row!" Muir shouted. The men put their backs into it, but the fog crept ever closer. Muir came and pulled me aside so he could be the one standing at the stern.

"If it wants anyone else, let it take me," he said.

The sinking ship gave out one last creaking wail, then with a hiss of steam it went under. The fog swirled and fomented above the spot. The tendrils retracted, falling back into a globular cloud that descended and sank with the ship, a last glimpse of luminescence showing in the night for several seconds before sinking into the depths, until it was finally too dim to see.

We drifted in a clear, calm bay under a blanket of cold night stars.

When news of this reaches the authorities, there will be recriminations and inquiries, funerals and wakes. But the one thing I will forever remember, the thing that promises to wake me in a cold sweat for years to come, was the conversation between Muir and Squire even as the lifeboat was rowed into the small harbor in Dunfield.

"I've failed," Muir said. "I got all those men killed."

Squire looked pensive.

"I'm not sure the brass will see it that way, old chap," he said, patting Muir on the back. "You didn't give us a means of defending our ships, that's true." He paused, and looked back out to sea, as if trying to mark the spot in his mind where the ship went down. "But it seems to me that you've developed a mighty efficient weapon."

3

Present Day

We all grew up knowing about the "fucker"—we didn't know what it was, but we sure as all hell knew enough to keep out of its way. At least I did after the winter of '96—before that I thought it was just another story told by old men with too much beer inside them, like the whale you could walk on, or the great white bear the size of a train that snaffled all the seals. I'd heard several variations on the story from men in various stages of sobriety and now that I had seen it for myself—again—I wasn't about to dismiss it, although I had no idea at all what it might be.

What I did know was that there was a protocol to be followed—all of the town workers had it drummed into us—any sighting of glowing fog had to be reported up the line immediately, if we wanted to keep our jobs. I left old George gawping at what was left of the plow blade and went inside to make the first call of what turned out to be a long spell on the phone.

I was put through to a government department in Toronto, and put on hold.

It took as long as it took me to smoke a cigarette down to the butt before they got back to me, but as soon as I told them where I was and why I was calling, things got moving quickly enough.

While I sat there with the phone to my ear listening to James Last's Orchestra murder a Beatles tune, I had George send

Jimmy Harkins out in the reserve plow with orders to keep his eyes open. He was going to have his hands full out on the highway trying to keep it clear with only the smaller-bladed plow, but it couldn't be helped. And I had to put it to the back of my mind as I was soon inundated with requests for information that I didn't have.

The folks in Toronto were most insistent in their questions about the fog. They asked where it came from. I didn't know. They asked where it was headed. I didn't know. All I knew was that it had made a mess of the heaviest sheet of metal in the area, and that I didn't want to get close enough to see it again. If they had asked me to go out and keep an eye on it for them, I was more than ready to tell them where to shove it.

Thankfully it never came to that. They said they had men on standby for such a situation arising, and that somebody would be with us soon. I wished them luck with that—I'd seen the weather forecast—nobody was getting on or off The Rock for a few days. Until then, we were going to be on our own.

After making that initial call I tried to get the RCMP team in Bonavista, but either they were too busy or the satphone was on the fritz again. I got through two cups of coffee and three more smokes before George came over to the radio desk. He looked as worried as I felt.

"Wind's getting up a tad," he said. "Should we get Jimmy to come back in? I feel bad about him being out there on his lonesome."

I nodded.

"Might be for the best—I shouldn't even have sent him out in the first place. This looked like it's settling in for a long stay. We'll lock it down for the night and get the highway cleared first thing in the morning—I'll put out the call."

I had another coffee as I did my duty and informed the rest of the island that our tip of the peninsula was closed for the night. A quick check online showed I wasn't alone. More than half the island's roads were currently closed to traffic, with more going dark every minute.

The Rock was hunkering down to wait out the storm.

From what I could see online, this storm was going to be one of the biggest in recent years. The satellite photo showed it sitting over the Grand Banks, the white spiral making it look like a gigantic snail, slowly making its way over toward Greenland. The national news was saying a foot of snow for us—the local boys in St. John's were calling for eighteen inches and more. My own guess was that we'd had about eight inches already, and possibly twice that still to come. Two feet of snow isn't a real problem—if it comes straight down. But when the wind gets up and blows it around, it's the drifting that causes issues, clogging up the hollows and trapping folks in their homes when it piles up against doors and windows. My team's job was to keep that from happening for as long as possible, and then to clean up afterward. Tonight, we'd skipped straight to the second option, our work brought to an early halt by the damage to the big plow. Now all I had to worry about was the return of the big bad thing from the old stories—and young Jimmy, who was out there with it.

"You called him in, right?" I said to George as he handed me a fresh coffee. The older man nodded.

"Sure did. He's out by the campsite and should be back anytime now."

I couldn't settle. I stood in the doorway, listening to the wind howl and watching the snow start to pile up across the road. It was only when I saw the lights of the plow turn into the depot yard that I allowed myself to relax—I'd had visions of Jimmy meeting the pale fog out on the open road, of the plow being melted and eaten with the poor lad inside. As I'd told George, I'd made a mistake sending him out in the first place—

the conditions alone had been enough to keep us all off the road, and Jimmy was prone to maneuvers that verged on the kamikaze while trying to cut corners to get the job done faster. If I hadn't been so shaken up on my own return, I'd never have sent him out—not in the smaller plow.

At times like this I hated being the titular supervisor. There were only the three of us in the crew for the small town—we'd had a lock on the tender for the last ten years now and couldn't see it changing anytime soon—until tonight. Now that I'd lost the use of the big plow, all bets were going to be off. I couldn't get distracted by that line of thought—there was too much going on, and the others would be expecting me to be on top of it.

We usually got on just fine divvying up the work without any need for me to pull rank on them, and George and Jimmy didn't need to be told to do anything twice. They rarely looked to me for direction—it only happened when the shit hit the fan, like tonight, and in this case, it was all going to be blowing in my direction.

I waited until the lad parked up and waved him inside before closing the door against the storm and anything that was foolish enough to be out in it. On any other stormy night, that might have been our cue to down tools and head for a game of whist and a few hours of well-earned sleep, but my experience at the road end and the subsequent coffee had me too wired to even think of rest. The other two seemed to pick up on my mood and left me well alone—George went to the microwave and started heating some pizza, and Jimmy went to the back room and switched on the television to the sports channel.

I sat at the laptop checking the *#nlwx* Twitter tag for anything out of the ordinary, and waiting for the phone to ring with bad news—in a storm like this there's always bad news from somewhere—it was just a matter of time.

Farther down the peninsula toward the main bulk of the island, Clarenville had its share of bad times already—they had power lines down in several places and three accidents on the Trans-Canada highway. I could only hope we didn't get that sort of trouble—without the big plow we would be hard pushed to deal with it.

When a call did finally come in, we didn't have far to go. Pat Finlay's voice was one of the most recognizable in town—as well as being the oldest man in the area, he also had the thickest accent.

"Get yersels down here, b'ys," he said. "The auld shed roof has collapsed and we need to get the boats out and somewhere else right sharpish."

At least the boat shed was just at the foot of the road from the depot, but that was the only good thing about the next half-hour.

Pat had been right—the boat shed—a building at least a hundred years old—had fallen inward under the combined weight of snow and wind. Only the fact that the roof hadn't completely caved in—yet—was saving the three boats inside from being crushed.

It looked like a lost cause to me—the seaward wall was already in the water and floating slowly away from us with the wind behind it and the side of the building nearest us was listing some three feet off the vertical. I wasn't totally convinced it was safe to be trying any work in the area at all, but the boats weren't just old Pat's livelihood—they were vital to the summer economy of the town. There would be an outcry if we didn't at least try to save them.

George sat in the small plow moving as much snow away as he could without causing more damage to the building. It wasn't going to be easy. The roof sat almost on top of two dinghies and a small crab boat. One of the dinghies wasn't salvageable, having had its rubber punctured in many places and the fiberglass portion of the hull cracked and broken into three distinct pieces. Jimmy and I managed to get a winch and strapping onto the crab boat and old Pat's pickup had just enough pull in it to drag the small vessel up onto the shore. Its bottom scraped hard on the shingle until it came up hard against the banks of snow and had nowhere else to go. By this time, the listing wall was at a perilous angle—if it came down—and it looked ever more likely it might—it could very well fall on top of us.

But that's why they pay us the big bucks.

I tried to ignore the danger and moved closer. The second dinghy proved more troublesome than the crab boat. It was the largest of the three vessels—a twenty-two-footer that was used in summers to take tourists up and down the coast on nature cruises. If we didn't get it out of the shed fast, it was never going to go any farther.

Old Pat climbed out of his pickup to supervise and George finally gave up on the plow and came down to give us a hand, but even with the three of us heaving and tugging, we couldn't get the dinghy to budge. It didn't look like it was wedged in anywhere but the sucker wasn't for moving anytime soon. The snow spattered in our faces, the wind whistled in our ears and my hands felt like I'd stuck them in an icebox for an hour. The tips of my fingers poked through holes in the left-hand glove, and it was just as I remembered the glass cracking in the plow door that I realized the light had improved—but not for the better.

I had my back to the sea, but I could tell from the look on old Pat's face that whatever was behind me wasn't anything I wanted to see.

"Don't look back, boy—just get yersel over here."

George and Jimmy had already started backing away up the small slope toward the road—George even beating the lad for speed despite giving away more than forty years. I had time to note that whatever was behind me was casting soft dancing shadows ahead of the departing men—then I felt it; a tingling at the nape of my neck. A high, sibilant whisper called out of the wind, voiceless yet strangely seductive.

"Come away, boy," old Pat shouted, and he too backed off quickly as the shadows got sharper and the tingling got more marked, as if I'd inadvertently touched a live wire.

I finally persuaded my legs into action and stumbled away from the dinghy as fast as I could manage. Old Pat's eyes went wide and stared at a point over my left shoulder.

"A bit faster might be useful," he shouted, and I took the hint. I was almost running as I reached him. I started to slide as I hit the slope, but Pat put out a hand, firstly to steady me and then to half-drag me up onto the road.

I turned to see the pale glowing fog hanging over what was left of the boathouse. I heard the whisper in the wind, louder now, more insistent, but felt no inclination to answer the call.

A fresh flurry of snow blew in my eyes. I brushed it away and, when I looked again, the fog was drifting away out into the bay. There was no trace of boathouse or dinghy in its wake, not even any debris, just a patch of clear water already starting to develop a skim of ice on top.

We stood on the roadway looking down into the water for long seconds before the howling wind and driving snow forced us to retreat. George half-heartedly offered to drag the crab boat farther away from the water, but Pat waved him away.

"It ain't coming back, boy. Not to the same place twice. Besides—we all saw the direction it took."

I hadn't mentioned it, but it had been in my mind. I nodded.

"It was making for Dunfield—back to the bay and the spot where…"

"Aye," Pat said, and spat on the ground at his feet. "Back to where it all started."

Jimmy was last to turn away.

"Did you see that? Did you?"

"Aye, boy," Pat said. "We all saw it."

"I thought it was just the auld folks trying to get a rise out of the young un's," the lad said as we led him away, heading for the depot, warmth and coffee.

Pat clapped Jimmy on the shoulder.

"A'body thinks that," he said. "Until they see it for themsel's."

I followed several paces back, lost in a memory.

I'd been as skeptical as Jimmy—once upon a time.

That had all changed for me in the winter of '96.

4

1996

I was twenty years old and all was right with the world. I had a steady job working for the town, I got engaged to Bettie Walker from Catalina at Christmas and now, on New Year's Eve, I intended to party hard with Joe and Harris Pollock, my best pals from school who were home from college for the holidays. Bettie wasn't happy—she had her hopes on spending a cozy night in with her folks, but I figured I had plenty of time for that in years to come. Joe and Harris had been in my life for as long as I remembered, and now I could feel them slipping away—who knew where we'd all be in a couple of years? I wanted one last night—marking the end of childhood was how Joe put it. I wouldn't have gone that far, but it did kinda feel like the end of an era, especially when we had arranged to meet outside the Bank—starting point for many adventures in summers gone by.

We walked down into the old town, passed the Village Inn without going in—there was a singsong going on over an accordion and fiddle combo. We weren't in the mood for the old songs that night—we were in the mood for jukebox classics and maybe a dance or two with any local lasses who'd ventured out for the festivities. That's why I thought we were headed for Rick's Bar and some games of pool to get the evening started, but the twins had other ideas. Instead of turning into the bar at the top of the next slope, they kept walking up and over the point to the far end.

"Where are we going?" I asked. "The beer is back that way."

Joe opened his jacket and showed me a full bottle of Screech.

"I've got the booze covered. It's a fine night. Let's take the boat out."

Fine wasn't a word I'd have used—it was a few degrees below freezing, and clear, with a sea of stars twinkling overhead. There was no wind to speak of, but I knew that out on the water even the slightest breeze would be apt to try to strip our skin off.

"Come on, guys—it'll be bloody freezing out there. I'd like to still have my balls attached in the morning."

"Is that so you can present them to Bettie Walker?" Joe replied, and dodged as I aimed a punch at his head that was only half in jest.

"Seriously—this is a bad idea," I tried again.

But the brothers wouldn't be dissuaded.

"One last adventure, for old time's sake," Harris said.

"Come on, Frank—all for one and one for all and all that happy shit," Joe added. "This might be our last night out together for a long time—maybe even forever if the jobs take us away after graduating. Let's do it right—just a quick spin out to the lighthouse and around the bay. We'll get some of this rum inside us, then head straight back to Rick's for a burger and the serious drinking."

When he put it that way, it didn't sound too bad and five minutes later I was helping them get their dad's creel boat out of the small, secluded boathouse in the sheltered harbor in the west bay.

Even then I thought they'd back out at the last minute—it was indeed as cold as I'd expected, and we were still inside the boathouse.

"Cast off at the blunt end," Joe shouted, and laughed loudly. Harris joined in, and that's when I knew they weren't going to be dissuaded. I decided to play along and see how far they were willing to push it. Maybe I should have tried to be the voice of reason for a while longer, but it was New Year's Eve, I was twenty, and these guys were my best friends in the world. Besides, adventure needs to be taken where you can find it—you never know how long it might be until you get another chance. I undid the ropes and jumped aboard as the boat started to drift out of the shed.

Harris turned the ignition, and I was still halfway hoping it would chug on an empty tank or flat battery, but the Honda two-stroke kicked in just fine, too loud in the quiet night. The three of us stood up by the wheel, Harris taking steering duties, as we headed for the lighthouse that marked the entrance to Trinity proper. Even in the dark we all knew we had to tack close to the starboard shoreline for a while to avoid the shallows. We passed the fish-drying decks and right on cue, Harris turned to port as we drew level with the old church. He pointed us straight at the mouth of the bay.

"First star to the right and straight on until morning," Joe said, unscrewing the rum bottle, taking a hit and passing it over to me.

"Not too far, please," I said, taking my first hit of the Screech and feeling the warm spiced rum hit like fire in my throat and stomach. "If we get in trouble, there's nobody around to get to us in time."

"Relax, boy," Joe said and clapped me on the shoulder. "Have we ever led you astray?"

The twins laughed at that, and I smiled ruefully, remembering the disaster that was our first visit to a local dance—the one where, at fourteen, we all got hopelessly drunk and were driven home in ignominy by the RCMP. Then there was the time we took my dad's pickup over the hill and burst two tires in a pothole—or any of half a dozen other occasions where a bright idea, usually from Joe, had only led to trouble. I wasn't blameless though—the three of us had always brought out the best—and worst—in each other. Judging by the rate we were getting through the Screech, I couldn't see tonight being any different.

I had to admit it was a glorious night for a sail. Harris cut the engine as we got level with the lighthouse and we drifted under as clear a sky as I have ever seen. The moon hung, almost full, just above the horizon away to the east, casting a silver path across the water with its reflection. The Milky Way was clearly visible in an arch above us, and Mars winked red off above Trinity itself. The outgoing tide slowly took us toward the harbor mouth and the Atlantic Ocean beyond, and the only sound was the lapping of waves on our hull.

It didn't even feel that cold—I was well wrapped up, and the Screech gave a pretense of warmth that was enough to stop me complaining. I was happy for a time, just drifting there, watching the reflected lights of the old town twinkle and dance in the water.

My calm didn't last though.

"Hey—we should go and check out the wreck," Joe said. "On a clear night like this, I bet we'll be able to see it just fine."

"That is the worst idea you've ever had," I replied, and turned to Harris for confirmation. To my dismay, he was already reaching for the ignition and turning the boat—not back to the town, but facing out to the open sea.

Joe handed me the Screech.

"Fifteen minutes each way—then straight back to Rick's and you get to decide what we do for the rest of the night. That's a promise. Deal?"

I took a long look at the town, turned my back on it, downed as much rum as I could stomach, then pointed along the shore toward Dunfield.

"Onward," I called. "And don't spare the horses."

I knew it was a bad idea, even before we passed Indian Head Rock and got to the more open water beyond. The cold bit deeper—even the Screech couldn't mask it, and we started to roll and yaw in a growing swell. But Harris knew these waters well—he spent most of his summers out in this same boat, hauling crab and shrimp with his old man. He handled the boat as if born to it, tacking back and forth across the waves, always heading straight for the gap that was just visible straight ahead—and the spot where all the stories originated.

The wreck was the stuff of local legend—a British battleship that sank in circumstances that could never be talked about, the theories for which ranged from "fucking aliens" to Nazi skullduggery, top-brass cockups to catastrophic accident. Whatever the cause had been, the wreck was obviously there—local fishing boats had to give the area a wide berth at low tide, and most of us chose to stay away from it completely, for it had developed an evil reputation in a very short space of time.

Of course, like the haunted captain's house on the hill above town, it was an almost magnetic draw for kids of all ages. We'd cruised around it—in this same boat—many times in our youth, looking for a glimpse of twisted hull, the hint of a skeleton—a shock or thrill that never came, until eventually we stopped coming around so much when the lure of beer and lasses proved stronger. This was our first time in the vicinity for several years—and our first ever at night in winter. The cold added an extra shiver to the one that ran down my spine.

Neither Joe nor Harris seemed to share any of the trepidation I was feeling. Now that we were out of the harbor and onto open sea, it felt like we were the only people in the world. The lighthouse winked at our back, but ahead of us there was only dark sea punctuated by solitary rocks. Tall cliffs loomed over us to starboard, lone stacks like shadowy sentinels watching our passing. Harris must have seen something in my face, for he laughed loudly.

"Come on, Frank, lighten up. It's supposed to be an adventure."

My sense of fun was fading fast as we got closer to the wreck site. The only adventure I fancied at that moment was chasing some beers after the Screech down into my gut, and my mood didn't improve as we sailed passed the Tern Rock and into Dunfield Bay itself.

At least here the swell died down and we had some signs of civilization—several lights showed in the houses on the far shore, reassuring me that we were not completely alone. Joe and Harris took lines of sight from the lights and the rocks on the horizon, and we sailed parallel to the shore for a bit before heading for deeper water. Finally, Harris brought us to a halt.

"Here—as close as I can judge it."

He cut the engine and we came to a standstill again. Apart from a slight swell, there was no sign of drift, and no sound but the gentle lap of wavelets on our hull.

"Okay—we're here. Job done," I said. "Let's go."

Joe leaned over the hull, peering into the black waters.

"Come and see," he shouted. "There's something down there."

Harris and I joined him in peering over. The boat listed so much that our noses were almost in the water, but I wasn't worrying about capsizing—all my attention was on what I saw beneath us.

At first, I thought it might be a sleeping whale—humpbacks are often seen lying still in the water in these parts—but not at this time of year. And humpbacks, as far as I knew, weren't luminescent.

Whatever was beneath us glowed—silver and blue and gray, shimmering like jelly in sunlight, just lying there, no more than twenty feet beneath us.

"Is that a bit of hull?" Harris whispered, but to my eye there was nothing that resembled a boat down there. The thing I was looking at seemed more like some vast jellyfish, hanging in the water waiting for prey to swim past—or float past, for even as Harris pointed, thin wispy tendrils began to wend their way up through the dark, as if tasting for our presence.

"Okay," I said softly. "Now can we go?"

Harris stepped away so quickly that the small boat rocked and yawed alarmingly, almost throwing all three of us off our feet. By the time I caught my balance, Harris had got the engine started, but Joe hadn't moved, standing at the stern staring at the sea. He seemed to be lit from below, the light throwing his face into skeletal shadows, his eyes sunk in deep black pits.

The light got stronger, brighter than the almost full moon, and for yards around us the sea glowed and pulsed as if alive.

"For fuck's sake, get us out of here," I shouted. Harris didn't need to be told twice. He throttled up the engine to full revs and we started to pull away. I looked back at the glowing patch of water—a light fog rose up from the surface, glowing faintly, hovering over the spot where we had just been. Fingers of wispy nothingness drifted in our direction, then were pulled back into the main body of mist.

We headed out of Dunfield Bay at full speed. I looked back just as we started our turn back around Tern Rock. The mist was still there, hanging in a dome over the wreck site, and as I watched, it seemed to collapse on itself and fall into the dark water until there was nothing left to see but the sea and the stars.

We didn't have a very happy New Year, all three of us doing our utmost to drink ourselves to oblivion, and mostly managing it.

This part of the story comes to a halt two days later. Joe and Harris asked me to join them in the boatyard. They had the creel boat out of the water and lifted up high on the trailer. I wondered why, until they showed me the hull—it was buckled and ridged—I know that wood can't melt, but God help me that's exactly what it looked like, like plastic that had melted, then hardened. In my mind's eye I saw the tendrils again, reaching for us from that glowing mass, stroking, almost tenderly, at the bottom of the boat.

I went straight back to Rick's Bar and made inroads into a bottle. It was a while before I came out again.

5

Present Day

When we got back to the depot, young Jimmy wouldn't shut up about what we'd seen at old Pat's boat shed.

"It was the fucker, wasn't it?" he said—and kept saying. None of the rest of us paid him any heed. We knew exactly what we'd seen. That didn't mean we had to acknowledge it—to ourselves or to anyone else. Jimmy paced the floor, buzzing with adrenaline and shock. The rest us of sat huddled round the wood stove, trying to get close enough to force some heat into our bones. George had got the bottle of Scotch out of his locker and we took turns pouring slugs into fresh cups of coffee.

"It's real, isn't it?" the lad said. "It's really real."

Old Pat lit a smoke before finally giving an answer.

"I've never been too sure of that," he replied. "I've seen it three times in the sixty year I've been here, and every time it's just like a wee bit o' fog, coming and going. It always takes something when it goes—and it sometimes leaves something behind too. All I knows is that I seen it—but I seen other things that's not real before now, so who knows?"

After befuddling us with that gem of personal philosophy, Pat went back to sucking smoke, and I sat there warming my hands on the coffee, trying to resist the urge to fill the cup with Scotch. The only thing that stopped me was the wind howling outside. The storm was still ramping up—and there would be more than old Pat needing our services before the night was out. The fog might be out there—but so was a town full of people, many of them elderly, sitting out the weather and hoping not to fall foul of it. It was my duty to keep watch over them, and that thought was enough to stop me taking to the bottle.

For now, at least.

I hadn't always been so strong, especially in those years just after our New Year's Eve excursion out on Dunfield Bay. I spent more time in Rick's Bar than was good for me—plenty more than was good for Bettie Walker. My engagement didn't last long, but I couldn't find it in myself to care too much—my head was always full of dark water and glowing fog. It haunted my dreams, it was there every time I closed my eyes, and only the oblivion brought on by booze gave me any respite at all.

And so it went, for three years—I held down my job, but only just, due to the forbearance of a kind supervisor and special dispensation for my encounter with the "fucker." The Pollock twins never returned from college, and I never heard from them again—nobody in town did. I often wondered if we shared nightmares, and if so, I hoped they were having a better time of it than I was.

Eventually, the dreams started to fade. I managed to sleep without too much booze, although I had developed a liking for it that proved harder to shift than the nightmare.

I got it all under control—or rather, I thought I had. But now it was back—and the thirst had come raging back with it.

"But we saw it," Jimmy said, bringing me back from my wool gathering. "We need to stop it."

"How do you suggest we do that," George replied. "We can't shoot it—and it's not exactly going to respond to harsh language."

Pat spoke again.

"As far as I know, it has never killed anybody," he said. "It might be best to just stay out of its way and let things take their course."

That sounded like a damned fine plan to me.

Jimmy kept prattling on for a while but I tuned him out. George and Pat made serious inroads on the Scotch—Pat mainly, for which I was thankful, for I might still need George before the night was out.

I kept checking the storm's status online. It wasn't going away anytime soon. The wind was up over a hundred kilometers an hour already, and was only going to strengthen. The snow, which had been heavy enough to start with, had decided to get serious, with accumulations in excess of three centimeters an hour forecast throughout the night. Without the use of the big plow, the town would be cut off from the highway in short order—might even be already for all I knew.

Around midnight the storm really started roaring. The next call came in five minutes into the new day—I recognized the voice, Margaret Brodie, a single pensioner in a big house at the far end of town just off the Bonaventure road.

"There's a big tree coming down out front," she said, as calm as you like. "It's looking to bring the power line with it too if it falls the wrong way."

I told her I'd be right with her.

Pat looked up, but I didn't need him—old men should be snug and warm on nights like this. That applied to George too—he was close to a well-earned retirement—but if it was the big tree I thought it was, then I'd need all the help I could get—Pat was going to have to hold the fort in the depot on his own. I told Jimmy to get the small plow ready and phoned Dick Hislett at the hydro depot to give him a heads-up.

As expected, Dick came on the line at the second ring. I told him what was what.

"I'll see you there in five," he said.

I remembered how bad the snow had been the last time I looked out.

"Best make it ten. See you when we see you."

I wrapped and zipped my coat and went out into the night again.

Just opening the door earned me an icy blast full in the face that had me seriously thinking about the pleasures of the Scotch bottle, but Jimmy was already halfway across the parking lot headed for the small plow.

"What do we need, boss?" George shouted from behind me.

"I'll take the big plow—the blade's no use but we can use its power and bulk if need be. Follow me in your pickup—we might need the winch."

He gave me a mock salute and headed for his truck.

If truth be told, I wasn't keen to get back in the plow's cab—not after the night's experiences—but George had called me "boss"—I'd better start acting like one.

Jimmy flashed his plow's lights twice to let me know he was ready and I led the three of us out. My lights only showed me ten yards or so of snow-covered road, but I knew this way well enough. There was a fresh six inches of the white shit on the ground, but, even despite being mangled and warped, the plow made short enough work of it, and Jimmy behind me took care of any that I missed.

We made good time down as far as the hollow at the campsite where I had to pull over and let Jimmy get the small plow at the drift that stretched the width of the road and some five feet high. I sneaked in a quick smoke while watching him work—it might be my last for a while.

To his credit, the lad did a fine job of clearing the road, piling the snow into evenly stacked walls on either side. It was only a matter of time before it drifted up again—this spot was notorious for it—but I hoped to be back in the warmth of the depot before then.

I led our small convoy to the far end of the road and Mrs. Brodie's house. There was no other traffic—no other sign of life, for the snow was thick enough to obscure my view of most of the houses, although they were only a few yards off the roadside, and I had my hands full keeping the plow on the road. The mangled blade had changed the driving dynamics completely, and now, when the wind caught the blade the wrong way, the whole rig tugged and pulled to the right, needing all my strength on the wheel to keep it straight.

I was happy to reach the road end with no mishap—but a lot less happy to see the tree ahead, leaning at a thirty-degree angle and looking likely to topple at any time. It was a big old maple, high, and thick in girth—more than a hundred years old at a guess, but not about to get any older. It had already pulled the earth up on the house side, brown earth showing among the snow. I hoped we weren't going to lose the water main too, but for then my biggest worry was the electricity.

I couldn't see them in the snow, but I knew that the power lines were only just overhead. If the tree came down, so would the line—and all the power in the town with it if we weren't careful. I didn't stop to think—I maneuvered the plow to line it up with the tree, raised what was left of the blade and put the rig's full weight against the leaning trunk. The cab shuddered, we slipped back six inches and I held my breath, expecting to have a face full of tree at any instant. But finally the brake bit, and we held position. Jimmy and George knew instinctively what to do. It was tough work with the wind and the horizontal snow, but we eventually managed to get a winch chain fitted around the trunk and had George's pickup take the strain. We'd ensured that we could control the fall but it looked to be only a matter of time before the tree came down.

"It's going to have to be moved," George shouted. "We can't leave it like this for long."

I agreed.

"And if it falls where it is, it'll take all the lines with it. We'll pull it over and drop it in the road for now," I shouted back. "We can shift it in the morning—there's nobody but us going to be coming this way till then anyway."

George nodded and got in his pickup. My plow pushed, Jimmy's smaller one pulled, and the winch chain tightened so much I thought it might start dragging on George's pickup, but his brakes held and the tree gave way under the strain. It fell slap in the middle of the road. I didn't even hear a sound above the roar of the storm, although there was a sudden flurry of snow that momentarily filled my view and blinded me. I had to get out of the cab to check, but we'd managed it—the power lines had stayed up.

I caught a glimpse of a light being switched on up the driveway at the house. Maggie Brodie came to her door and waved, beckoning me toward her. I trudged up the slight slope through nearly a foot of snow.

"I've got coffee or soup if you boys need something hot?" she shouted.

At that moment, coffee sounded exactly what I needed.

"I'll get the lads," I yelled back, and turned, walking away. My shadow, cast by her hall light, danced and flitted in the snow. As I reached the end of the short driveway, the shadow got darker, and the snow around me took on a pale glow. I'd seen that glow already that night—I knew what was behind me.

It took all of my willpower to turn back—just in time to see the glowing fog settle over Maggie Brodie's house.

6

From the journal of Duncan Campbell, 15th July 1955

Well, I'm back—back in the one place in the world I hoped never to set eyes on again.

It's not as if I had much of a choice in the matter. Last Wednesday I had a visit from old Muir. He's not the man he used to be—browbeaten and battered by the military brass in their attempts to get him to divulge the secrets of his "experiment." He'd stuck to his guns this past year and more now, but when he arrived in my Chelsea flat that night, I saw something new in his eyes—it looked like despair.

"They won't let it be, Duncan," he said as I poured him a stiff drink. "They want a weapon—and they won't believe me when I tell them that I have no idea how to build it. You saw what happened in Dunfield—it was a bloody accident—a terrible, terrible accident. All I did was put the pieces in the right order, at the right time, in the wrong place."

"You've tried again, then?"

He nodded, and gulped at his drink.

"Several times to no avail. They think I'm swinging the lead—that I'm some kind of conscientious objector. But you know that isn't me. I just can't get the bally thing to work. But I have an idea."

I had a sinking feeling in my gut—I didn't want to hear what he had to say. I sipped at my Scotch, hoping that he'd take my lack of interest as a sign to keep quiet. But keeping quiet has never been Muir's way—and he hadn't changed quite that much.

"I want to go back, Duncan. It won't be official, so I can't force you to come—but I'd like you with me. I want to have a good close look at that wreck."

That was possibly the last thing on Earth that I wanted—I was still having nightmares from the last time—but I felt responsible for my own part in last year's proceedings, and Muir was most insistent. When he mentioned that his intent was only to put things right, and not in fact an attempt to give the military what they wanted, I agreed, reluctantly, to accompany him.

When I woke in the morning, I realized that the Scotch had been doing my talking for me, but Muir had already accepted the fact that I was on board. As it turned out, he already had all the preparations in place. All I had to do was get on a plane—three planes actually, then a bone-rattling car trip across the island from Deer Lake airstrip to Trinity.

But all the discomfort of the trip was forgotten as we pulled into the old town. The memories of that fateful night came flooding back. The last year may as well have only been yesterday.

I'm sitting here now, late on the evening in The Village Inn. I can hear Muir in the bar downstairs, arguing loudly with someone. I can't say the locals are pleased to see us, for the memory of last year's disaster is as raw with them as it is in myself. We need a boat—but I am not at all sure that any will be forthcoming.

From the journal of Duncan Campbell, 16th July 1955

Well, I was wrong about the boat—Muir didn't exactly win the locals over, but his money proved to be more persuasive than his arguments. We have the use of a creel boat for as long as we need it, but we have not, as yet, managed to retain the services of anyone to pilot it for us. That meant a comical hour after breakfast as Muir and I took turns going around in circles in the harbor to get the feel of the craft while trying to avoid crashing into anything or grounding ourselves on hidden shallows—of which there are many. Such was our ineptitude that local children took to standing on the old harbor wall shouting abuse and laughing at our pitiful attempts at seamanship, and it was almost noon before we got up enough gumption to leave the relative safety of the harbor.

We headed out, in as straight a line as we could muster, to the lighthouse at the mouth of the bay, then along the coast toward our destination.

The clear sky and bright sunlight seemed to mock my apprehension. We had a spot of lunch—grudgingly provided by the innkeeper—while moored just off Indian Head Rock. A solitary bald eagle eyed us from the top the whole time, ready to swoop should we discard any morsels of food. After eating, we lit up smokes before continuing.

Muir seemed almost happy. We had talked several times in the past year, but neither of us had much of an urge to discuss that night out in the dark and fog—the horrors were all too raw, all too real. But now, out in the bright sun and sparkling sea, something impelled him to broach the subject.

"I have been thinking, Duncan," he said.

I laughed.

"Don't strain yourself, old man."

My attempt at levity wasn't appreciated. Muir continued without acknowledging it.

"I am coming round to a theory—if you'd like to hear it?"

I waved for him to continue. Anything that kept us from approaching Dunfield Bay was fine by me at that moment, and I was rather enjoying the feel of warm sun on my face.

"We know much about the internal structure of the atom and how to effect changes in it," he said, lapsing into his *professorial* voice. "But what if there is more than just fission and fusion for us to play with? What if we could stretch the empty space between the nucleus and the electron shells? We would, in effect, be making the very structure of matter thinner, more diffuse. Think about it, Duncan—is that not what we saw that night?"

"I try not to think about it," I replied, but Muir wasn't to be dissuaded. He continued without waiting for further reply from me.

"What if what we stumbled on was a new way to manipulate the very basic structure of matter itself—and without any risk of explosion or radioactive fallout? What if…"

This time I interrupted him.

"Perhaps we should have talked to that crew about risk before we started."

That brought him up short.

"It is in the nature of the advancement of science that…"

"Please don't," I said. "There is no justification that I will be willing to listen to. Not this close to where it happened. If you are determined to see what a mess you made, then let's get to it. Perhaps then you will realize the folly of following any further course of action in this direction."

I am afraid that things between us were rather strained for the rest of the short journey along the shore to Dunfield Bay.

We arrived at the site in mid-afternoon. A slight breeze ruffled the bay, reminding us that July in Newfoundland is still perilously close to winter at times, but the bright sun continued to keep much of my lingering gloom at bay.

Muir stripped down to a pair of trunks, a mask and a snorkel.

"It's going to be bloody freezing down there, man," I said. "This is madness."

"Don't worry, old boy," he replied. "I'm a bit of a dab hand at this. If I can do Orkney in November, I'll be fine here. I'll be back in five minutes, tops."

He tipped himself overboard without another word, going in with a splash that was the only sound in a suddenly quiet bay. The small boat rocked gently side to side, then fell still. Even the handful of birds sitting on the Tern Rock went quiet, and the scene, in my mind at least, took on an air of quiet anticipation.

My hands were shaking as I lit a smoke, but the simple act that I repeated many times a day did much to anchor me back in reality. Muir bobbed to the surface twice over the next few minutes, just long enough to get a snorkel of air before descending again into the black depths. I tried looking over the side, but the water was too turbid, only allowing me a view of the top three feet or so.

My imagination went into overdrive, providing me with images of ghostly rotting hulks where reality was not all that it seemed, of spectral arms reaching for Muir as he swam through murky water, of a glowing fog that ate all in its path. I almost screamed when Muir bobbed up at the side of the boat without a warning and dragged himself aboard.

When I saw what he had brought up with him, that scream came even closer.

It had been a fish—once upon a time. Or at least I think so—the tail end sported a definite fin, and there was another along the length of its back, although that was more wispy and webbed than any I'd seen before. It was the head end that was going to give me nightmares for many nights to come though. It looked as it if had been melted, then stretched and pulled, teased out into a fringe of almost snake like appendages, before being hardened back in place. Everywhere you looked there was something not quite right—a piece of eye too near a jagged bony area that might once have been jaw, scales on what had been a tongue, and tiny suckers that looked more octopus than fish that ran along the whole length of the body. The colors were all wrong too—an oily sheen that was almost iridescent, blue and green and yellow all at once, the whole effect being one of an unnatural sickness. At the end of each…tentacle, for want of a better word…a tiny mouth opened and shut, gasping for respite from the air, eager to be sucking water.

"Throw it back, Muir, for pity's sake, throw it back."

Far from being repulsed, Muir seemed fascinated.

"She's still down there, Duncan," he whispered. "Mostly in one piece too. And there's fish all over her."

"That's a fish?"

"What else could it be?" Muir said, bending over the thing. "It's what I was talking about earlier—the stretching of reality at a base level—creation at its most primal."

"It's an abomination," I replied.

"No," Muir said, wrapping the thing up in a wet towel. "It is evidence. And I intend to delve deep into its secrets."

We barely spoke on the way back to Trinity. I did most of the steering—he could scarcely take his eyes off the wrapped bundle on the deck at our feet.

He's out there now, in the shed behind the inn—*delving*.

I want no part of it. There's more going on here than I feared, and meddling with it is not going to improve matters.

Our course of action cannot lead us anywhere I want to be, but for tonight, I intend to stay far away from that thing in the shed. I shall drink Scotch, smoke cigarettes—and pray to God that I am wrong.

7

Present Day

Maggie Brodie was little more than a shadowy figure in her hallway, lost somewhere inside a sheath of glowing fog that enveloped the whole house. I took a step back up the drive, intending to go to her aid, but was stopped by a hand on my shoulder.

"Don't, lad. Just don't."

George had a firm hold of me, and didn't intend to let go.

Maggie—already noticeably dimmer, and somehow unnaturally thin, screamed, the sound barely reaching us through the wind. I tried to shuck George off me but he belied his age and held on tight, even as Maggie clearly tried to force her way toward us through the increasingly thickening fog.

"Let me go!" I shouted.

"She's gone, lad," George shouted in my ear. "Look at it. Just look."

Maggie had stretched—thin to the point of emaciation, her left arm little more than a wisp of shadow, her head long and oval, like a squashed egg. Her mouth opened, a black hole containing only darkness—and then she was gone, lost inside the shifting glow.

Even then I fought against George's grip. I'd known Maggie all my life—from church on Sundays as a lad to her damned fine cakes and pastries, from her numerous letters to the town council in her neat, tight, hand to her too-careful driving in the town's streets that infuriated the younger lads in their flash pickups. She couldn't be gone this easily. She just couldn't.

"Come back, lad," George shouted again. "It's looking to take us too."

The fog swirled, drifting, against the wind down the driveway toward where we still stood. I finally allowed George to drag me away, back to the road, then right up against the side of the big plow. Jimmy was off beside the smaller vehicle somewhere to our left by the fallen tree, but I couldn't look in that direction—I only had eyes for the fog, inexorably coming forward, an inch at a time, as if feeling its way by touch.

Despite the wind and the snow, I felt a hot tingle across my face like sunburn that was gone as quickly as it came. The wind dropped suddenly, as if a switch had been pulled, and the fog lifted up and away from us before coming loose and diffused. I blinked, looked again, and saw only the flat gray of low clouds above us.

I turned to check on young Jimmy. He was staring, open-mouthed up the driveway. I followed his gaze—it wasn't just Maggie Brodie that was gone. There had been a solid, two-story house on the spot a minute before, but now there was just an empty lot. Where the building had been, was a flat sheet of thick ice, as if a large amount of snow had melted, then frozen immediately.

Dick Hislett arrived in the hydro truck just as the wind and snow ramped up again. The big man squeezed himself out of the tight fit in the cab and waddled toward us. Swaddled up in a thick parka and weatherproof trousers, he looked like a small bear coming at us through the storm.

His first thought was for the tree.

"You can't leave that there," he said, then saw where we were all looking and did the best double take I've ever seen outside the movies. "What the hell happened?"

"It's back, Dick," George said. That was all he had to say. Dick Hislett's face went as white as the snow around us.

"Oh, shit. We need to get out of here. We need to evacuate."

"Tell me about it," I replied. "How's the road to the highway?"

Hislett couldn't take his eyes from the frozen lot that was all that was left of Maggie Brodie's house, and I had to give him a nudge to get a reply. He turned to me and I saw fear dancing in his eyes.

"Damn near impassable," he said finally. "We'll need the big plow."

"We'll have to do without," I said. I turned him round to point him at the rig. "I met the fucker earlier. It was out on the highway—so I'm thinking—where the hell are we going to evacuate to?"

Dick looked from the mangled blade, to me, then back to the blade again.

"We can't just do nothing," he started, then stopped, thinking.

"You see the problem?" I replied. "We're in the middle of a fucking storm, almost everybody is in bed—and if we try to move out, we're likely to get ourselves—and anyone who comes with us—killed anyway."

"But we can't..." Dick said again.

"Yes, we can. We just need to keep an eye out, be ready to move fast and react—it's not as if that isn't what we do anyway."

There was fear in Dick's eyes again as he looked over to the vacant lot where the Brodie house had been.

"You mean to keep people on the move—out of its reach?"

"It's the only thing I can think of—until the cavalry get here. But in this weather, I don't think we should rely on any rescue. We're on our own."

The four of us got into Dick's pickup for a confab. They all looked at me—it seemed I was the designated boss for the night. I knew I was going to have to get the council involved before I went much further, but for now, these guys needed something immediate, something to stop them from thinking too much about the Brodie house and what might happen again at any moment.

I kept my gaze on the road ahead as I laid out what was going to have to do as a plan.

"We take a quarter of the town each," I said. "Keep the main road through open as much as we can, and stay in constant communication. If we see anything—if that fucker comes back—we get the nearest householders out of its reach, and keep moving on."

"That's it?" Dick said. "That's your plan?"

"You got a better one?"

He went quiet, but I saw he wasn't happy. George and Jimmy seemed to accept my idea though, which was enough to be going on with. I assigned them each a patch of road. I knew full well that in a couple of hours my plan would be overtaken by conditions in any case.

But I had to do something.

"Call in every ten minutes. And we meet at the depot," I continued. "Every hour, on the hour. Let's try to keep everybody safe and get through the night."

Dick grabbed for his radio even before the rest of us left the vehicle. George and Jimmy headed out into the storm but I stayed where I was in the passenger seat. I knew Dick well enough to know that he wouldn't scratch his ass without permission—he was going to try to get his office to bail him out.

The radio crackled and hummed, but he got no reply from the other end. He tried his cell phone, but the signal out here is ropy at the best of times, and he had no more luck than he'd had with the handset.

"Looks like you're stuck with us, Dick," I said. "You take this end, from here to as close to the highway as you can get. That way you'll be first to see the cavalry if they turn up, and first to make an escape if the weather lifts."

If he heard any slight to his bravery in my voice, I was long past caring. I left him in the pickup and headed for the big plow.

I put Dick to the back of my mind—either he did his job, or he didn't. I couldn't take the time to worry about him when I had a town to look after.

I'd given myself the peninsula—the oldest part of town nearest the water. I figured the "fog" was most likely to come off the sea—I based that conclusion on a hunch more than anything else, but I was running on nervous energy and intuition anyway, so another guess wasn't going to matter much.

The road was mostly clear on the way over, Jimmy and George having gone ahead of me, but fresh drifts were already beginning to build mere minutes after their passing.

This is going to be a losing battle.

The big rig rocked and bucked below me as a gust of wind took us side-on and threatened to topple me over into the draining ditch. It took all my strength to hold a straight line. I drove down through town to the bank, parked up and tried to contact a councilman—any councilman.

The only one I could get was Wayne Robertson. He sounded groggy at first, just barely awake, but got his head on fast when I brought him up to speed.

"I'll head out and rally the troops. We'll get the Anglican church hall open," he said. "Bring anybody there that wants to come."

I felt slightly happier with the situation, knowing that somebody else had taken up some of the heavy lifting. I put the rig in gear and headed out to see what else the night might throw at me.

The streetlights were still on. That was about the only good thing about my drive along and over the peninsula. It was only a couple of hundred yards, but the wind and the rig both fought me every inch of the way, and my arms ached from having to maintain a rigid grip on the wheel. The warped blade threw nearly as much snow back on the road as it cleared—but at least I was able to make progress, albeit slowly.

The radio crackled as I passed Rick's Bar, mercifully saving me any lapse into memory and sentimentality. It was Jimmy, checking in.

"Nothing to report down at the theater end, boss. She's piling up fast though—don't know how long I'll be able to stay out in this."

"Just keep at it, boy," I replied. "And keep your eyes open for...you know what."

"Ten four, boss. Heading up to the bank and over to see if George is okay. Speak to you in ten."

George was very much alive, though not particularly happy. He checked in just after Jimmy signed off.

"I'm just outside the funeral home," he said. "Damn near got stuck in Giffords' driveway, and Woods Lane has an eight-foot drift across the entrance, so there's nobody going that way for a while. No sign of the fucker though, so that's something."

"Yep—that's something all right. Any word from Dick?"

"Nope. I went down toward the turnoff a couple of minutes ago, but it's drifting up right bad in the dip at the campsite again—it'll be impassable in half an hour."

"Do what you can," I said, realizing just how futile our puny attempts seemed against the force of nature raging around us. I wondered if the glowing fog had any sense of our presence at all? Did it even register us—or were we no more than snowflakes, dashing ourselves to oblivion against it without even being noticed?

I was woolgathering. George had spoken again, and I'd missed it.

"Say again," I said.

"Do you want me to try for the gas station? See if Dick's down that way?"

"No—leave him. He'll shout loud enough if he sees trouble—at least we can be sure of that."

The radio fell quiet and I was left alone again in the wind-rocked cab.

I tried Dick on both radio and cell phone, but got only static on the first and no signal on the other.

He's a big boy—he can take care of himself.

I went up the small hill at the west end of the peninsula doing no more than four miles an hour, almost driven backward by the wind before I pushed the pedal and put the full weight of the rig into it in an attempt to get over the top. Snow spattered the glass in front of me and once again the wheel kicked and bucked, as if trying to throw me out of the cab.

I wrestled control just as we topped the hill and started down—too fast now, sliding and slipping with no traction beneath us. I grounded the blade and put pressure on the brakes at the same time—not too fast, else I'd have toppled right over. Something screeched below me and we slowed—but not enough. The bottom of the hill was coming up fast where the road turned and headed back round the point to town.

I wasn't going to make it.

The plow headed straight for the ten-foot drop-off into the bay below.

I put caution to the wind and slammed on the brake, hard. The rig turned sideways and slowed down, but not nearly enough to stop the inevitable. I banged the blade hard into the bank at the side of the road and scraped snow in a long furrow, slowing us even further. The blade dug in, turning and pulling the plow around so that we were now going almost backward.

We were still heading for the drop, which was coming up fast.

I'm not going to be able to stop her. We're going over.

I kicked open the door and threw myself out into the storm, rolling and tumbling in fresh snow as the rig fell away and disappeared from my view.

8

From the journal of Duncan Campbell, 17th July 1955

I woke at six a.m. with an epic hangover and a thumping that wasn't all in my head. Muir stood outside my bedroom door, hammering loud enough to wake everyone at the inn.

"Get some clothes on and get out here, Duncan. Quickly, I need a witness."

By the time I got partly dressed he was already bouncing up and down with excitement at the top of the stairs. His hair was tousled, as if static electricity had run through him, and his eyes were wide with excitement as he tugged at my arm, almost dragging me along the corridor.

"Where's the fire?" I asked.

He kept tugging.

"Hurry, man. It's going fast, and I need someone else to see it."

My heart sank as he led me down through the inn and into the old shed in the small garden at the back. He had a shelf under the main window set up as a makeshift laboratory. His traveling case lay open at one side—small microscope, slides and a selection of scalpels, scissors and tweezers. The "fish" from the day before, lay sliced open on a slab of slate. I didn't want to take a closer look, and I tried for flippancy in the hope that Muir might let me go.

"It's a fish," I said. "I've seen one before."

Muir pulled me closer to the shelf.

"Look at it, Duncan. Just look."

Every fiber of my being wanted to turn away, but I forced myself to step closer, enough that I could look down at the thing.

It wasn't quite dead, despite having been splayed open from chin to tail fin. The fringe of tentacles wafted slowly above the slate, as if tasting the air.

"I know it's only a fish," I said, half turning back to Muir. "But you could have had the decency to kill it first."

Muir pushed me over until I was inches away from the thing.

"Do you think I did not try? The guts, Duncan. Look at the guts."

I looked for the guts, but saw nothing resembling a digestive system. There was a mass of amorphous tissue, blue and green and silver all at once, writhing and squirming—almost worm-like. A cloud drifted off, allowing a shaft of direct sunlight to come in through the window—and that's when I saw it. An aurora of dancing color—like a rainbow of vaporizing oils—hung over the dissected thing, drifting slowly in a slight breeze.

I backed away fast and covered my mouth.

Muir stood at the door, smiling.

"I thought you'd like it."

I dragged him outside and gulped in some fresh air.

"Get rid of it—burn it now. You don't know what kind of contagion might be coming off that...that... thing."

"Nonsense," Muir replied. "I've been working over it all night, and I'm none the worse for it. But did you see? It's not just the external appearance of the thing that has changed—the whole internal structure has been modified. Yet it still lives! Is that not the most wondrous thing you have seen?"

"*Wondrous* is not a word I would use in this situation."

Muir had stopped paying attention to me. His gaze was at a point over my shoulder, back in the shed. The sunlight fell full on the thing on the slate, and it was burning up beneath it, bubbling and foaming, oily, almost soapy, bubbles forming, swelling and popping. The air above the shelf filled with dancing, swirling hues of blue and red, green and orange, rising up in a thick cloud before being torn and shriven by the breeze until all that was left was a blackened, tarry mass on the slate.

"I need more samples," Muir said.

"What you need is some rest, man. Tell me you haven't been at it all night?"

He smiled.

"Don't try to mother me, Duncan. I'm a big boy now. And don't fret—I raided the inn's pantry twice during the night, and I'm swimming in enough coffee to sink a boat. And talking of which—come on. We need to go back out. I need to find the cause of the transformation we've just seen."

He was not to be argued with, and I wasn't about to let him go back to the wreck on his own. I did, however, insist on having breakfast, which turned out to be a light one, for the sight of what had become of that poor fish had quite put me off my grub for the time being.

We went back out in the creel boat—just the two of us again, but we felt much more comfortable handling the vessel than we had the day before. Muir had managed to purloin several dozen empty shrimp and lobster cages and had stacked them perilously high on the deck. Yesterday's calm was replaced with a stiff breeze and a swell that was getting heavier by the minute. The boat seemed to be handling it well enough though, and besides, I had other things to worry about.

It seemed that Muir had developed a new obsession. His last one had led, on a direct, clearly defined path that could be traced afterward, to the disaster that night in the bay.

Where in hell will this one lead us?

"So tell me, Muir," I said, lighting up a smoke as we passed the lighthouse and left Trinity Bay behind. "What do you hope to find?"

"An answer, Duncan. Maybe the only important answer—something has managed to bend matter at the most elementary level. I mean to find out what that thing is—and to uncover its secrets."

He wasn't in the mood to stop and explain further. We cruised past Indian Head Rock at full throttle, and reached the spot over the wreck again in mid-morning. He wasted no time in stripping for action, and went over the side, taking two of the lobster cages with him.

Once again, I was left alone with the sea and the gulls for company. I lit another smoke and tried for calm, but now I was thinking about dancing colors, and oily sheen. I was thinking about contagion.

If Muir had any qualms, he did not show them. He dived and came up again half a dozen times, on each occasion bringing up his samples. There were deformed fish, something that looked like a mating of crab and octopus, and something else that looked like a sponge but gave off more of the iridescent vapor as the sun hit it. What with those, and a great many shells that might once have been mussels but were now soft, stretched and deformed into grotesque parodies of themselves, we had a full boat as we started off back to Trinity.

Muir is down there, hard at it again, in the shed. He has asked me to join him, but I believe I shall stay here and reacquaint myself with the Scotch bottle this evening.

It seems like the safest course of action by far.

From the journal of Duncan Campbell, 20th July 1955

Despite my protestations and refusal to give him any help whatsoever, Muir has been back and forth to the wreck three times now, and each time he returns more excited than the last. I fear he may have bitten off more than he can chew. I must put a stop to this, and soon.

But how do I go about it? That is the question that is vexing me now.

That blasted shed has become the focus of all Muir's activities—his laboratory, if you will. Apart from two hours' sleep, or fewer each night, and the trips to and from the wreck, he has been bent over his samples this whole time, scarcely speaking a word to anyone, let alone me.

The locals are also getting restless. Although the true story of what happened that night out on the bay last year has never been disseminated, and was clamped down on by the powers that be, there have obviously been rumors spread in the town. These tales have been wild and strange in many cases, yet some are far closer to the truth than the tellers might imagine. Muir's activities in the shed are only serving to fuel those rumors, and it is only a matter of time before someone pulls him up on it. This can only end badly.

As I have said, Muir is oblivious to anything but his work on the samples. He allowed me access for several minutes this afternoon—a brief respite that I insisted on, having fetched him a pot of coffee and some pipe tobacco.

At first he would not permit me entry—he came out into the sunlight and sat on the seat in the garden as we shared the coffee and lit up a pipe each. He looked tired, near exhaustion, but there was a gleam in his eye, as if he was onto something big.

"How goes it, old man?" I asked.

"It's all rather fascinating," he said. "I've found something that will shake the foundations of the world, Duncan—I have opened a doorway to the wellspring of creation itself."

I put that down to hyperbole and tiredness at the time, but now I have to wonder—especially after he allowed me a glimpse into the shed. He had one of the things he'd brought up in a long glass tank—the thing that may once have been a crab—or an octopus—but was now a grotesque amalgam of both. It scuttled, clacked, squirmed and roiled against the glass, leaving behind an oily rainbow residue that hung in the air for a second before subsiding to the floor of the tank. Muir had been most careful to put it in a shaded spot and it was all I could do to stop myself from dragging it out of the shed and letting the sun get at it.

Muir pushed past me and went back into the shed.

As he closed the door, the sun came out from behind a wispy cloud. I hope to God I imagined it, but I fear I did not. Just as he closed the door, I saw rainbow iridescence rise in a haze from his bare forehead.

9

Present Day

I got to my feet gingerly, all too aware that I had come close—too close—to going down into the icy water with the rig. I peered over the edge, having to cup my hands over my eyes to avoid them being filled with stinging snow. The plow lay mostly submerged in eight feet of freezing water, waves lapping over the clearly visible crack in the side-door window. The headlights sputtered and went out, and the rig rolled slightly, settling another two feet deeper. Access to the spot was going to be impossible without a heavy crane and a boat or two—there was no way the plow was moving from this spot until spring at least. At that moment, I couldn't say that I was particularly bothered—I was too busy counting myself lucky to be alive.

I turned my back to the wind and checked my pockets—I had smokes and an old lighter—but no cell phone—it too was down there in the water, beyond retrieval.

I checked my arms and legs—in this cold it would be all too easy to miss a bad cut or even a break, but it seemed I had landed softly enough to avoid any injury. I pulled the hood of my jacket up, over my face and forward over my brow. Turning my back to the wind and bending my head forward gave me a hollow where I could get a smoke lit—it took three attempts to fight the trembling in my hands. I stood there for nearly a minute, buffeted by wind and snow and not caring as I sucked the smoke down deep and tried not to think about how close I'd just come to being frozen solid until spring.

I couldn't hang around feeling sorry for myself. The other guys would be checking in about now, and panicking when they couldn't reach me. If I knew Jimmy the way I thought I did, he'd be on his way in this direction pretty damn soon. I had to stop him making the same stupid mistake that I just had. I started back up the hill, following the track the plow had made on the way down. It was already starting to drift up, little trace left of my headlong rush toward oblivion only minutes earlier. At least the wind was at my back, hurrying me along as I climbed.

I couldn't hear anything but wind whistling in my ears, couldn't see anything but snow whirling like dervishes around me and spattering against the back of my coat like rapid gunfire. Cold bit at my feet and ankles, which felt heavy and tired already. I tried to up my pace, aware of the very imminent danger of exposure and death.

Then I remembered that the fog was also out here somewhere.

I was almost running by the time I went over the top of the hill—too eagerly, for my feet went from under me and I slid a good ten yards down the other side, arms and legs akimbo, before coming to a stop in a fresh drift.

At least I was slightly sheltered in the hollow where I'd landed, but I couldn't afford to delay. When I tried to push myself upright, pain flared in my left shoulder—something was busted in there—I had to roll onto my side and use my right arm to get myself up—taking three attempts before getting to my knees. The wind seemed to laugh at me as I staggered down toward Rick's Bar.

By this time my only thought was to get inside as soon as possible. I tried to peer through the storm, looking over the town to see if Jimmy's plow might be on the way to my rescue, but there was nothing in my view but more snow.

Rick's Bar it is then.

The bar lay in darkness, and the door was closed, but I was in no mood for niceties. I put my good shoulder to it, hard, twice, and it gave way beneath my weight. I slammed the door shut against the wind and leaned back against it, waiting for heat to find me and for my heart to stop thudding in my chest and ears.

The bar's landline got me through to the depot on the first try, but I got no answer. There was no answer from the church hall either—although there I got a continuous busy tone that gave me hope that somebody was actually on the case and doing something about the situation.

I breathed deeply, tried to relax, and started to assess my situation. At least I didn't seem to be in imminent danger, although the storm seemed to be strengthening if anything. The whole structure of the bar creaked and rocked in the wind, and even after I switched on the main lights, there was a sense that any feeling of security might only be temporary, as they flickered alarmingly, in danger of giving up on me at any moment.

There's something about an empty bar that gives me the creeps. When the place is busy—or even just when the lights are low—there's a feeling of intimacy, good company, and happy memories. But go there alone, under the full glare, and you'll see the faded carpets, ripped seats, nicotine stains and the faint smell of piss and stale beer. It reminded me too much of years that I'd never get back again.

And woolgathering wasn't going to help any.

I helped myself to a glass of rum—a large one, thankful for the heat in my belly—and tried every number I knew, and some that were written on the wall beside the phone. I got no answer anywhere, and that's when I really started to worry. They hadn't had time to get everybody to the church hall—not yet, in this weather. Somebody, somewhere should be answering. The fact that they weren't had me thinking again, of the glowing fog, tendrils like grasping tentacles, and Maggie Brodie reaching for me as she slipped into the dim depths.

I really wanted to just lie down on one of the pool tables and go to sleep. The bar was warm, protected, and safe, for now. But my town was in trouble. I might not be in the best shape to do something about it—but it looked like somebody had to. I downed the last slug of rum and put the bottle back in its place behind the bar. It called to me, but not strong enough to take hold. I knew that, if I made it through the storm, there would be other calls in my future that I wouldn't be able to resist so easily—but for now folks needed me.

I wrapped myself up as tight as I could manage—I found two hooded sweatshirts on a hook near the door that were too big for me but gave me some much-needed extra padding under my fleece coat. I pulled the hoods as far forward over my head as I could, closing them with the drawstrings so that I only had a small opening to look out of.

As soon as I opened the door, I was almost blown back into the bar. I bent over, put my good shoulder into the wind, and headed back out into the howling storm.

The wind had veered, coming more from the east—all that meant was that it was colder still, picking up chill air—and speed—as it howled across the Atlantic, first stop Newfoundland. I shuffled, scuttling almost crab-like and tacking against the gale, heading down the slope toward the old part of town, taking care with my footing—my shoulder ached bad enough without having me land on it again.

I started to make out streetlights. The first house I came to was Alistair and Janine Connors' place, tucked in the hollow at the turn at the foot of the hill. There was a light on in the front window, just visible through blowing snow, and I couldn't in all conscience walk on by without checking on them.

With the wind at my back, it meant I was almost running as I went up their driveway. It was immediately obvious something was wrong. The front door lay open, snow piling up in the hallway, so deep I had to climb over it to get inside.

"Alistair. Are you here?"

At first, I hoped they had merely left in a hurry, perhaps having been taken to the church hall. But the television was on in the front room. A weather report told me that we should expect a storm as I went through the back and into the kitchen. I stopped for a second in the doorway, struggling to comprehend what I was looking at.

The Connors had obviously been at supper when they got a visitor—the rear wall of their kitchen showed the same partially melted then hardened look I was coming to recognize. What had once been a granite worktop was now a ball of stone in the corner; the range had melted and fused into the exterior wall, and the glass of the window was buckled and bulging, throwing distorted fun-house reflections back at me. I crossed the room to check on another melted pile that looked to be the remains of a table, chairs and a cabinet, now all fused and melded into a grotesque pile of junk. There was no sign of Alistair and Janine among the wreckage, and I was starting to hope that they might indeed have made their escape. That was before I opened the door and looked out onto the back porch.

They'd tried to make it out—that much was obvious. But it's hard to run when you're embedded in the decking from the waist down. It was as if the wooden boards had opened up and then closed again, hard and fast. Alistair's waist looked too tight, too pinched. Blood and gore ran from his mouth down over his chest, half-frozen, glistening in the light that came from the kitchen behind me. He'd been squeezed to death—and he'd fought it, I could see that by the blood and the strips of flesh he'd flayed from his fingertips. I could only imagine how long it had taken him to die there, in the cold, snow blowing in his face, impossibly caught on his own back deck.

Janine had gone easier, as if that was any consolation—there was no blood, no sign of struggle. When the wood took her, she'd slumped forward, head first.

Her face was completely embedded in the hard decking.

My next conscious thought came to me as I stood outside the depot, banging as hard on the door as I could manage, so cold I couldn't feel my hands, so tired that I fell into old Pat's arms when he opened up to see what the commotion was about. I let him half-drag, half-carry me to a chair by the stove.

I began to feel more myself when he poured coffee into me—it tasted more of rum than anything else, but I wasn't complaining. When he offered more, I took it gratefully. I pushed myself as close to the stove as I dared and got a smoke lit with hands that took twice as long as normal to obey my orders. The taste of the tobacco reminded me that I was alive—it was only then that I thought to ask after the others.

"Has anybody called in?" I asked.

Pat nodded.

"There's a confab going on at the church hall—George headed over to see what's what. Jimmy's still out on the plow—

he went a-looking for you down at the harbor about five minutes ago—he should call in any second now."

"And Dick?"

Pat shook his head and spat on the stove, the spittle dancing and hissing as it vaporized.

"Not a peep," he said. "George tried to get down that way not long after you all left, but it's drifted up bad at the campsite. If Dick's down there, he's staying there."

"Then I need to get to the church hall," I said, and tried to stand, but my legs were having none of it and I sat back down hard in the chair before I fell over.

"You're going nowhere for a while, lad," Pat said. "I've seen men who have died of exposure—and they all looked like you did when you got here. You're lucky to be alive—just stay there and get warm. What will be, will be."

My brain was still trying to catch up with me. Memory was coming back—of a headlong flight with the wind at my back, running and falling in almost equal measure, pain in my shoulder, cold in my feet and hands, and nothing in my head but that single image—Janine, face melted into the wood of her porch deck.

We'd had a barbecue on that deck just last summer—half a moose, ten crates of beer and as much rum as we could get down us, late into the night laughing and joking and singing the old songs. That had been my memory of their porch—one that I'd never revisit—it had been supplanted by the horror I'd just seen, the horror I hadn't quite managed to blank out and which was even now creeping back.

"You saw it again, didn't you?" Pat said softly.

"No—I didn't see it—but I saw where it had been."

The old man didn't prompt me, but I started to tell him anyway—he particularly enjoyed the part about me trashing the big plow, but went quiet when I got to telling about what I saw on that damned porch.

"Both of them? Alistair and Janine?" he whispered.

I nodded again and sucked smoke for a while.

"We need to get out of here," Pat said after a time. "We're sitting ducks."

I'd had this conversation already, with Dick in the hydro van—no doubt I'd be having it several times before the night is over.

"We've no heavy gear, and the main road is blocked—ten feet high by now in the hollow, I'd guess."

"But we can't just sit here..."

I interrupted.

"We had a plan—quartering the town and keeping our eyes open. That didn't help the Connors much, did it? The cavalry is on its way—well, the government boys anyway. As long as we keep our wits about us, it might be best to sit it out."

Pat wasn't too keen, I could see that, but he was also old enough to know better—trying to run anywhere in this storm was a sure way to get yourself dead.

George arrived back just as I was starting my second smoke.

"How was the meeting?" Pat asked, as he made his way straight over to the stove.

"Not good," George replied. "The 'fucker' has taken a dozen folks—and that's a low estimate, they think. Half the town is in hiding—hunkering down in their basements and cellars—and the other half is over in the church hall." He turned to me, and I saw fear in his eyes. "They're going to do something stupid—and our lad Jimmy is egging them on—they're going to make a run for the highway."

10

From the journal of Duncan Campbell, 22nd July 1955

The locals have asked—rather, demanded—that I intervene with Muir. They have become increasingly worried about the direction Muir's so-called research is taking, and Muir himself isn't helping with his high-handed attitude toward their protestations. The last straw for them came last night.

Muir had not left the shed all day apart from making some rather strange requests of both the innkeeper and myself in the morning for the supply of copper wire, crystal valves and an array of acid batteries. I didn't know what he wanted with the gear—I only knew that no good would come of it. The innkeeper had to send to Clarenville for some of the items, and a pretty penny was going to be added to our bill on our eventual departure, but Muir seemed unconcerned at the cost, and continued to demand that all haste be made to procure his requests.

He eventually took delivery of the goods at the shed door, opening it just enough to allow passage of the items inside, not enough for me to get a glimpse of what he was doing. I got a good enough look at the thing in the tank again though. It had grown—or should I say, it had developed. It was the size of a cat, and there seemed to be more of the octopus about it now, and less of the crab, although there were four eyes on crustacean stalks, and a single massive claw that looked more than capable of having a man's arm off.

In the late afternoon I gave up watching the door, and headed for the bar, where the innkeeper and I were the only patrons. I got a potted history of the town, he got the brunt of my frustration at Muir's pigheadedness, and together we got through the best part of a bottle of some of the local firewater. Rum, he said it was, but it tasted like nothing I've ever drunk before, hot and spicy with a distinct treacle-like aftertaste. I developed rather a liking for it over the next hour or so.

It did have one other effect I was thankful for—it dropped me into a deep, dreamless sleep as soon as my head hit the pillow in the early evening.

When I woke, it was dark, and I was disoriented for several seconds trying to remember where I was and what I was doing there. I rolled over and stared up toward the ceiling, watching the play of light and shade. A shimmering rainbow aura lit the room, sending shadows dancing. I felt a tingle—like pins and needles, but crawling all over my body—it was a most unpleasant feeling indeed. Blue light flashed, then again, and the shadows danced and capered faster than before. I knew immediately who must be the cause of this light show.

Muir! What the blazes is he doing now?

I dressed quickly—almost too quickly for I almost tipped over trying to get my leg into my trousers and just missed smacking my head off the wardrobe. I had enough foresight to pick up my smokes from the bedside table, then left the room at a run, heading for the back garden.

Half a dozen of the locals were out there already, having obviously just left the bar—some of them were still carrying their beers—but no one was drinking. They stood on the back porch of the inn in a huddle as if unsure whether they should get any closer to the shed, which was indeed the source of the light show. No one spoke to me as I joined them—I'm not sure they even registered my presence; the lights were more compelling than I could ever be.

Irregular flashes of blue light blazed inside the shed, casting outlines around the door and windows and even showing through where board butted against board in the wooden walls. A rainbow shimmering danced across the roof, like thin smoke that refused to dissipate in the breeze, but insisted on clinging to the building. Most eerily of all, there was no sound—I heard the breeze, the startled exclamations from the men on the porch at each new flash, but the shed itself sat strangely quiet.

"Where's Muir?" I asked the innkeeper. Of all of us on the cramped porch, he stood closest to the shed door, as if he'd attempted to step into the garden, but turned back at the last moment. He didn't reply, merely cocked a thumb at the source of the light. And he didn't try to stop me as I stepped off the porch and onto the trodden track through the grass that led to the shed door.

"Muir," I shouted, my voice sounding too loud. "Are you in there?"

The blue light blazed again, so bright I had to avert my eyes. The rainbow aura on the roof thickened into more of a fog.

"Muir. You must stop this nonsense."

I put my hand on the door, intending to push it open.

And stared, uncomprehending, as my hand, wrist and most of the forearm went straight through it, as if it was no more than a projected image.

I do believe I might have let out a yelp of surprise. I tried to pull my hand away, expecting at any instant that the door might become solid, trapping me there, bound to the wood. Even as I started to step back, a hand gripped mine from inside the hut and dragged me forward. There was the strangest sensation of lightness, as if I might have bobbed like a balloon on a piece of string. I saw the door come toward me, felt a shiver and tingle rush through my whole body, then I was through, standing inside the hut with Muir gripping tight at my hand.

"Try not to touch anything else," he said. "There's a good chap."

I turned back and gingerly put a hand on the door. It was solid once again, and I was able to open it and look out to see the startled faces of the men on the porch. If they had thought to come to my aid, they had not yet done anything about it. I waved at them to show I was not in any immediate danger, and closed myself back in the hut with Muir and his equipment.

A glittering contraption of copper wire, coils, crystal valves, batteries and roughly cut pieces of wood and metal sat on the long work shelf. It gave out a blinding flash of blue light from the valves as I noticed it.

"Don't look directly at the light," Muir said. "It leaves one with a stinking headache."

I looked around the shed.

Muir had totally commandeered it for his "experiment"—apart from the strange device on the shelf, he also had numerous cages and boxes filled with biological samples, the largest of which was the strange crab-octopus hybrid I'd already seen. The beast in the tank was scuttling and slithering with what seemed to be excitement as it bathed and luxuriated in a thicker section of the dancing rainbow aura. It had got larger again—pretty soon Muir was going to need a bigger tank.

"What are you trying to achieve here, man?" I asked. "The locals are getting ready to run you out of town."

"Let them try," Muir said. "This is Nobel-winning territory, Duncan. I believe I have discovered a way to access the most basic building blocks of reality itself—the stuff of primal creation—a gateway to the secrets of the universe."

I did not quite know how to reply to that; I certainly suspected it of being more of Muir's hyperbole, but it was clear that he believed at least some of what he had said. I turned my back as the contraption on the shelf pulsed blue again, so intense it was brighter than the sun, even through my closed eyes. Muir patted me on the shoulder a few seconds later.

"Open your eyes, Duncan. Look here."

I looked where he pointed. It took several moments for my eyes to adjust to the glare, and I had to squint. Even then, it wasn't actually clear what I was observing, but there was obviously something happening.

A tear in the fabric of space, no bigger than a sliver of fingernail, appeared above the work shelf and hung there. As I watched, it settled into a new configuration, a black, somewhat oily in appearance droplet little more than an inch across at the thickest point. It seemed to be held quivering in midair by some strange force emanating from Muir's makeshift contraption.

It looked like an egg.

Muir looked like the cat that had got the cream, a broad grin plastered across his face.

"We did it, Duncan. How does it feel to be a god?"

I looked at the black egg, then Muir, then back to the egg again. The rainbow aura thickened again, dancing around the shimmering thing that hung impossibly real in the air above the work shelf.

I knew exactly how I felt.

Bloody terrified.

"What in blazes is it?" I whispered.

"Think of them as soap bubbles." Muir replied. "Reality consists of many of them—multiple, maybe even infinite, universes, each in its own bubble, each connected by the thinnest of membranes to many of its neighbors. Quantum foam, if you like."

It made more sense for me to think about them as eggs, if truth was to be told. Maybe I should have let Muir die back in the wreck of the boat, that dark night out on the bay. Maybe it would have made a difference. That's what I was thinking about when I turned away from the shelf to face him.

"So, what happens now?"

"Now we study it. Think of it, Duncan. A whole new universe at our disposal."

"And what's inside the bubble?"

He laughed.

"That's what we're going to find out. Of course, all we know about space and time may or may not apply on the other side of the field boundary. No one has ever done this before."

"I'm starting to understand how Oppenheimer felt," I said.

His smile faded as quickly as it had come.

"Don't you dare go soft on me. Not when we've come so far together."

He was right—we'd done this together. I was just as culpable as he was for what was done in our name.

I had another look at the egg.

Had it grown?

It certainly looked larger to me. The shed started to throb, like a heartbeat. The egg pulsed in time. And now it was more than obvious—it was most definitely growing larger.

"The field boundary is collapsing," Muir shouted.

The throb became a rapid thumping; the shed shook and trembled. The vibration rattled my teeth and set my guts roiling.

A blinding flare of blue blasted all coherent thought from my head. When I recovered enough to look back at the shelf, there was nothing to be seen hanging there but empty space. The black egg was gone as quickly as it had come.

"Quite impossible," Muir whispered, talking to himself. He was staring right at the spot where the egg had been.

"What did you see?" I asked.

"For a moment there I thought—no, it can't have been."

"Muir, you're not making any sense."

He looked at the shelf again, then back at me. He seemed to come to a decision.

"The boundary collapsed, that's all. We need more batteries to sustain a more stable magnetic field. We'll try again tomorrow. But we're close, Duncan. We're nearly there."

When I left the shed, it was to face a barrage of questions from the men on the porch. I had no real answers for them, and I fear my attempts at dispelling their very real concerns might have been halfhearted at best.

"We all saw you," the innkeeper said. "You went through that bloody door as if it wasn't there. You can't stand there and tell me that's natural."

"I can assure you..." I started, but was interrupted. The big innkeeper poked me in the chest with a stubby finger, punctuating each word hard enough to cause me some degree of pain.

"No. You can't assure me of anything."

They mean to give Muir an ultimatum sometime soon, and if he does not comply, they intend to make him leave by any means necessary. Mention was made of putting a torch to the shed and its contents.

I am by no means sure that is a bad idea.

11

Present Day

By the time we struggled down the road to the church hall we were too late to stop Jimmy from giving false hope to the folks gathered there. There was a crowd of around fifty. I knew every one of them, but they looked at me as if I were a stranger—and a foreign one at that—when I tried to dissuade them all from heading out into the storm.

"Yes, Jimmy has the plow—but it's not the big one—we lost that—and the hollow at the campsite is going to be too deep—it'll take him half an hour and more to clear it. And that's only if the snow stops and the wind drops now. Meanwhile the snow will keep drifting up on the parts where he's not working, and you're all going to get stuck in it. Add in the weird shit that's going on around here tonight and it's madness to even think of trying."

Jimmy, despite being one of the youngest adults present, seemed to have been appointed spokesman and leader.

"It's madness to stay," he said, almost shouting. The rest of the hall fell suddenly quiet around us—we had everybody's attention. I'd seen the school bus in the parking lot on the way in—and the pickups, some of them loaded with suitcases—and even furniture. Some folks were intending to leave for good. And Jimmy had their blood up—along with his own.

"You saw what it did to the Brodie place," he continued. "And it's done for the Connors, the Fothergills and old Mrs. Johnson down by the bank. How many more, we just don't know. We'll take our chances with the weather—at least we know what's what with that."

There were murmurs of agreement around the room, and nobody would meet me in the eye. It seemed that minds were already made up—but I gave it one more try.

"I've called it in. The government men are on their way…"

I didn't get to finish. Jimmy shouted me down.

"And what use are they going to be? Even if they get here before we're all taken, what are they going to do? What can they do? As old George said earlier, it's hardly going to respond to harsh language, is it?"

That had me stumped. What we were dealing with was so far beyond my ken that I could not even visualize what might be done about it. I only knew about snow and wind—and I knew enough to know that there was no chance of any escape from either until they'd both settled down for a spell. My mouth spoke before my brain was ready.

"They're scientists—they get paid to think shit up," I replied. I realized just how lame I sounded. At least nobody laughed. But when Jimmy turned toward the door, everyone present apart from Pat and George started to follow him.

I collared Councilman Robertson at the door.

"Don't go along with this, Wayne. These people need leadership, not spur-of-the-moment decisions."

He pushed me away.

"What they need is to get the fuck out of here," he replied. "I saw what happened to the Connors—if you did too, then you know what I'm talking about. I'm not going to let that happen to my family—not while there's a chance of getting to the highway."

He turned away before I could protest further and headed for the door.

"At least check in with us at the depot," I called after him, but he didn't acknowledge that he had heard me. The rumble of engines starting up was loud even above the whistling wind of the storm.

I didn't bother going outside to see them off—I'd seen idiots driving in heavy snow before. Seeing more of them was just going to depress me.

We left a note in the church hall in case anyone else came along, and the three of us headed back to the depot. It took us twice as long as it had on the way down, fighting the wind every inch of the way and trudging through snow that was more than a foot deep in places on the road. I looked up every ten steps or so, hoping to see the lights of a returning convoy, but there was only the biting flurry of wind-whipped snow and the dim orange of the almost obscured streetlights.

Fifty souls had gone out into the storm—I was worried that far fewer than that would come back—if any.

At least the depot was secure and warm—warmer still after George got me some fresh coffee. Pat and George looked near as bad as I felt—pale, almost ashen, and tired enough to sleep the day around. But all three of us knew that sleep was a luxury we couldn't afford just then. I lit a smoke and watched the radio, willing it to squawk at me, desperate to hear that Jimmy had proved me wrong.

All we got was dead air.

My shoulder ached, I was cold down to my bones, and I'd seen more than enough horror to do me for one night. But I couldn't settle, couldn't live with the knowledge that I'd let all those people head off into the storm so ill-prepared. I let it slide for almost an hour—until around four in the morning—the dead hour, they call it—then I couldn't take it anymore. I stood, too fast, the resultant dizziness threatening to put me straight back in the chair.

"Where do you think you're going, young 'un?" Pat asked.

I waited until the room stopped spinning before answering.

"Out to the campsite—if they're still there, they'll need some help—and if they've got through, then we all can. Either way—I need to know."

The old man looked me in the eye.

"I can see that you do. But you said yourself—it's not a night to be out gallivanting."

I buttoned up my coat and pulled the hood down over my eyes.

"I'm going anyway—I need you two to stay here—stay sober and man the phone and radio. I'll be back in twenty—either way."

George looked up from his seat by the stove.

"And how are you going to get out to the site, lad? You already trashed the big plow, Jimmy's in the other one, and the gritting truck won't get through—not now."

I'd already thought of that—I didn't like the idea, not one bit, but it was the only plan I had so it would have to do.

"I'll take the Skidoo."

George laughed.

"Good luck with that. It's not been out of the shed in two years. It probably won't even start."

As it turned out, the snow sled did start. We had to dig out a three-foot drift at the shed door just to get to it though, and I was weary and sore even before I sat in the saddle. George had helped with the digging—he also helped me get the Skidoo out of the shed and into the parking lot. He passed me a pair of heavy-duty gloves and a set of goggles.

"You'll need these. Just do me a favor—don't get dead."

I gave him a mock salute, kicked the beast into gear, and became one of those idiots who go out into snowstorms.

It wasn't a far ride—only four hundred yards or so—but it felt like it took forever. I could barely follow the tracks made by the small convoy—an hour's fresh snow had all but filled them in—but I knew the way well enough. The Skidoo bucked and rolled in the wind, like a small boat on a rough sea, and I was tossed around like a sack of potatoes, bringing fresh flares of pain to my shoulder with every bump. Visibility was down to ten yards or so, and I was afraid to push the sled to its top speed—if I hit a drift just wrong, I'd be in it for days before anyone found me.

I passed two houses with lights shining in their porch, but most of the rest of the dwellings along the road had gone dark. I had no time to investigate, pressing on as fast as I dared, hoping against hope that Jimmy had pulled off a miracle and got them all out.

That hope was dashed as soon as I turned the corner that led down into the hollow in the road by the campsite.

They were all there—what was left of them.

They had found the fog—or it had found them. All that was left of the plow was a blob of fused, melted metal and glass, down in a partially excavated drift at the deepest part of the hollow. The plow had been reduced to a rough three-foot cube in size; I hoped to hell that young Jimmy hadn't been inside—although if he had, he'd have gone quickly. That might in itself, have been a blessing, given what had happened to the others.

Vehicles were strewn across the hollow—some in the road, others deep in snow on either side, having tried—and failed—to escape. All had been melted and fused—but to differing degrees. Some, thankfully, like the plow, had been squashed and deformed beyond all recognition. But others hadn't taken the full brunt of what the fog was capable of.

The school bus was worst—it was still recognizable as a bus—and there were obviously people inside, faces pressed against the windows where they too had melted and fused until it was hard to tell where skin began and glass ended. Heads and torsos were stretched and distorted into impossible lengths and shapes, all frozen now, icy statues, a testament to their folly. I recognized many of the faces though—even distorted as they were, they were still folks I'd talked to every day—folks I'd never see again.

I forced myself to get off the Skidoo and check anyway—there was nobody alive in the hollow but me—in some ways that was a mercy. But many of them had died hard—as hard as Alistair Connors, with blood at their mouths and fingers, or with faces contorted in the agony of having their every fiber stretched beyond what was humanly possible. I'd seen a kid's doll burned in a lighter flame once—this looked almost like that—limbs elongated and melting then hardening into something almost monstrous. I gagged, nearly lost what little food I had in my stomach, but kept it down—this time.

I found Wayne Robertson—what was left of him, at the seat of the school bus, his lower torso sank deep into the vehicle's floor, with the steering wheel embedded deep in his head. He hadn't managed to escape the fate he had so dreaded.

It took me twenty minutes to check the wreckage before I was completely sure no one had survived. By that time, I was close to just lying down and giving up—the wind threw me around, my legs felt like two bags of cold concrete, and the snow spattered so loud against the goggles I couldn't hear myself think. I knew I should get back on the Skidoo—hightail it out of there and back to where I could start to feel warm, feel human. It was as if I was transfixed—I could only stand and stare at the melted ruin of the convoy—my townspeople—in many cases my friends.

It was a while before it occurred to me that I was the only one currently with any possibility of escape. I had the Skidoo—it would get over or around the drifts in the hollow, and get me at least as far as the highway. I could be off and away, out of here in minutes.

I dismissed the thought as soon as I had it—I couldn't live with myself if I did, and then discovered that those I'd left behind had suffered the same fate as these poor souls in the hollow. My dreams were going to be bad enough as it was without adding any more misery and horror.

I did, however, have one thing I wanted to check out—Dick was still out here somewhere as far as I knew—we'd left him just past the hollow down at the Bonaventure turnoff—only a hundred yards away past the drifting. I got back on the Skidoo, pointedly ignoring the carnage all around, and gave the throttle a kick, enough juice to get me up and over the drift.

I crested it a second later, the wind kicking me in the torso almost hard enough to dislodge me from my seat. The Skidoo skidded to the left, chugged twice and came to a halt.

I peered down from the top of the drift toward the turnoff. There was light there for sure—but it wasn't Dick's headlights, or the lights from the gas stop. This was more diffuse, glowing as if moonlit from within. It didn't take long for me to realize what I was looking at.

The fog lay over an area the size of two football fields, clearly visible despite the blowing snow. It seemed to crawl—against the wind—heading slowly in my direction.

That wasn't what impelled me to throw the Skiddoo back into gear and hightail it back to town though. What caused me to flee in a funk was the sight of what happened to the three people I saw down there, trying to push themselves through the snow away from the fog.

"Hey," I shouted, but if they heard me, they paid me no heed, concentrating on their attempt to escape. I couldn't recognize them, heavily swaddled as they were in winter clothes—two looked like adults, the other one maybe a small woman or a teenager—what was apparent was that they were all terrified.

I kicked the Skidoo around and tried to get the engine going. It coughed twice, three times, then took. I pointed it toward the small group, intent on going down to their aid—but I was already too late.

It got the smaller one first. A tendril of mist seemed to waft lazily out of the main body—little more than smoke. But when it curled around the fleeing figure's torso, it was with enough strength to drag him or her off their feet. They were dragged back into the main body of the fog so quickly that if I'd blinked, I would have missed it—there was only the memory of a body disappearing into the glowing mist that seemed suddenly strangely thin and elongated.

The second went three steps forward later, dragged by a tendril around the ankle to be pulled, arms waving frantically, snow being thrown in all directions, struggling to no avail.

The larger figure lasted longest. He found a shallower area of snow, put his head down and headed at a run toward me.

"Come on. Come on," I shouted.

He reached the side of the road, slipped, almost fell, and steadied himself by grabbing around the trunk of a hefty conifer that marked the entrance to one of the houses. Or rather—he tried to. His arms seemed to go through and into the wood itself, along with his right shoulder and half of his chest. He raised his head to yell in alarm, just as his head and the tree trunk merged into one.

And it was only then I recognized him—Dick wasn't going to be making his escape—he wasn't going to be doing much of anything except dying hard. The fog shifted slightly, and the wood stopped melting, hardening again, leaving his head and upper body completely embedded in the thick trunk. His free arm beat hard against the wood, twice, and his legs kicked and thrashed.

It was several seconds before he went still and limp.

That was when I fled.

12

From the journal of Duncan Campbell, 23rd July 1955

As it turns out, the locals have not had to make good on their threat to put the torch to Muir's work—he has managed to bring about its ruin all on his own. It has been quite a day—I have a bottle of Scotch beside me as I write this, and most of it will be gone ere the conclusion, so forgive me if I show a tendency to ramble as this account goes on.

As I said, it has been quite a day—and it started early. On this occasion, it wasn't Muir who woke me up—it was our innkeeper. He was most apologetic at waking me at the ungodly hour of six in the morning, but he said he had something that I had to see—something impossible, or so he said.

I was still rather bleary as I followed him downstairs and out onto the porch.

"I saw this as soon as the sun came up," he said. "I was standing in the kitchen getting the breakfasts going, I looked up—and there it was."

At first, I didn't see what he meant—until a cloud moved aside and let slanting morning sun flood the garden.

A rainbow aurora, like oil shimmering in the sun on a hot day, hung over the stand of birch trees, swaying in time with the waft of branches in the breeze off the sea. It was all very pretty, but the sight of it filled me with deep dread and I felt a shiver of cold despite the summer sunshine.

"It's your man, Muir's doing, isn't it?" the innkeeper asked.

"I'm afraid so," I replied.

"Then you can tell him from me," the man said. "If he doesn't stop what he's doing today, there won't be a shed left by nightfall. You two are my guests here—it would do you well to remember that."

It seemed the fabled Newfoundland hospitality only stretched so far—although to be honest, I was surprised Muir had got away with it for this long.

"Why don't you tell him yourself," I said.

"I would if I could. Your friend left early—took a loan of my cleaner's truck and headed out. He said he had supplies to gather. He's headed for Catalina—about fifteen miles up the coast. He'll be back by lunch at a guess. You can tell him then. And there's something else you need to see."

He led me across the grass and up to the shed, stopping some eight feet away from the door as if afraid to approach any farther.

"We all saw what you did yesterday," he said, his voice barely a whisper. "You went right through the bloody thing. So, I went over earlier to see how the trick was done. That's when I found it." He wiped his fingers on his shirt, as if trying to remove some ingrained dirt. "Go on, touch the door. You'll see what I mean."

He didn't move to join me as I walked up to the door. Remembering the day before, I was somewhat more circumspect this time around. I stretched out my hand and let my fingertips touch the wood—gently, almost a caress. Even so, it was enough for a piece of the door to turn to dust under the pressure, as if it were no more than a structure of ash and splinters. Where the dust fell, a dancing rainbow accompanied its fall to the ground.

"And that's not all," the innkeeper said from some way behind me. "He's got some kind of animal in there—and I don't think it's too happy about it."

Inside the shed something scurried and slithered, and there was a loud clatter I could only imagine as claw against glass. I was in no mood right then to do any further investigation. I stepped back gingerly to once again join the innkeeper.

"The whole shed is like that door," he said. "One good gust of wind and it'll be gone. What in hell has your man done in there?"

I wished I knew the answer to that one, but we were both equally bemused as he invited me back inside for a spot of breakfast.

A mound of eggs, bacon and toast washed down with strong coffee did much to improve my mood. When I joined the innkeeper for a smoke on the front porch, the sun was already warming up the day nicely, although neither of us felt the need to broach the topic of what we'd seen out back at the shed.

I was quite content to sit and watch the world go by—although in truth there was not a lot to watch. Trinity has become a sleepy, somewhat neglected town in this day and age, a sad comedown from its former glory as one of the largest whaling ports in North America. There were no whalers now—scarcely even any fishermen, and I smoked two cigarettes down to the butt before anyone passed the front of the inn. I said hello to a woman and her young son. The lad smiled back at me, but the woman gave me such a look—you'd have thought I was a mass murderer. It seemed that Muir's reputation—and my own alongside it—was growing fast—and not for the better. My attempt at finding a good mood to enjoy had failed almost before it got started.

I considered taking a stroll around town, not having anything else with which to occupy my time, but the call of the shed was alluring and enticing. It was not long before I was once again out in the back garden, standing on the porch and watching the light and play of shadows in the garden and on the shed.

The rainbow aura above the trees was more pronounced than it had been earlier, and when the sun fell on a patch of grass to my left, a distinct dancing haze of color rose in the heat. The innkeeper was right to be concerned—there was no knowing what side effects might ensue—might already have ensued—from Muir's headlong rush toward enlightenment.

I walked around the shed, keeping a good six feet between it and myself, studying it from all angles. Now that I knew what I was looking for, I saw shifting rainbow color everywhere, roiling and dancing betwixt sun and shade, thick, almost like smoke, above the shed itself.

Blue light flashed at the window—not as bright as the day before, but more than enough to be noticeable.

Had Muir returned without me having noticed?

I walked over to the window, having to stand on tiptoe to see inside, being careful not to touch any of the shed itself for fear of it crumbling under my fingers.

The blue light came, as I expected, from Muir's contraption on the shelf. The strange amalgamation of copper wire, valves, wood and metal gave out a constant glow, and a resonant hum I could feel in my gut and at my jaw even here out in the garden.

The rainbow aura was everywhere, flitting and dancing around the interior, touching on shelves, sample jars, walls—and it was especially thick near the long glass tank, where the crab-octopus hybrid seemed to bathe in the aura's attentions.

It had grown even bigger—the fish tank was not going to be able to contain it for long now—the tentacles were now near as thick, and longer—than my arm, and the single claw was thicker still, black as pitch and looking as sharp as any razor. Even as I watched, four stalks rose from the main body, and four beady little eyes turned toward my location outside the window.

The bloody thing knew I was there.

I stepped back involuntarily, and almost went down on my backside. I put my right hand down to steady myself. The grass was brittle to the touch, and when I rubbed it between my fingers, rainbow-hued dust spread in the breeze.

I was sitting on the porch smoking the last of a succession of cigarettes when Muir returned just after noon. The bed of the battered pickup truck was laden with his purchases.

"Give me a hand, would you, old chap," he said. "Some of this stuff is rather heavy."

He was right about that—there was a battery that must have weighed several stone on its own, more reels of copper wire, and several large sheets of corrugated iron alongside half a dozen lengths of two-by-four timber.

"What in blazes do you intend to do with this lot?" I asked.

"We need more power," Muir replied. "I need to stabilize the field boundary—and for that, I need to make a larger containment chamber."

Larger was not a word I needed to hear right then—it got me thinking about the grotesque hybrid creature in the fish tank—that was certainly something that should not be allowed to get any larger than it had already become.

I helped Muir lug the contents of the truck through to the back of the inn. We left it on the porch while we had a rest and a smoke, but Muir was clearly itching to get back to his work.

"The locals won't stand for it, you know," I said, trying to keep my tone light and non-adversarial. "They want you to stop—and I'm pretty sure they're serious in that request."

"Stop? Nonsense," Muir replied. "As I said—we are close to understanding the phenomenon, and when we do, it will make us famous. It is historical work on par with any done this century—perhaps even more so, for we are dealing with the very nature of existence itself. How can I stop now when I am so close?"

"Nevertheless—we are guests here, Muir," I replied. "It would be extremely ill-mannered to ignore their concerns."

"Bugger manners," he replied. "This is no time for outmoded methods of thought. Come, man, let me convince you further—let me show you wonders."

I know I might have protested harder and longer, and I might have done more to persuade him of the error of his ways. But Muir was as much a force of nature as the very things he was attempting to control in the shed, and I have never been able to refuse him once he gets his dander up.

And this afternoon, his dander was at a high point. I followed him over and into the shed.

There was something inside I had not been able to see from the window. A black, almost oily egg hung in the air above the work shelf. It gave off a distinct hum—the same as I'd felt in my gut and jaw earlier, stronger here than outside, and an accompanying vibration that made me more than slightly nauseated.

Muir had a look of relief on his face.

"It has stabilized," he said, and smiled, but I wasn't falling for it this time.

"So let's say I believe you, and it is indeed stable," I said. "In that case, what's got you so worried?"

He sucked on a pen as if pretending it were a cigarette.

"I wasn't going to tell you," he said eventually. "It might be nothing. It was something I saw when the field collapsed yesterday."

"Just tell me," I said, cold terror gripping me again. I wasn't at all sure I wanted to hear his reply.

"It was just when the field went," he said. He couldn't look at me. "And only for an instant. But when the field collapsed, I thought I saw the egg burst. It opened out—a fine, rainbow-infused fog. It seemed to swell and diminish, twice, as if breathing, and when I looked back, it was gone."

"Fog?"

"Probably an effect of the field itself—you know, like the patterns you can make with magnets and iron filings?" He sounded like he was trying to convince himself rather than me.

"A burst bubble," I whispered. "A fractured universe, if your theory is indeed correct. Anything at all could have happened. We're damned lucky to still be here, aren't we?"

He nodded, and looked pale. He pointed at the floating egg again.

"But look, it's stable now." It sounded like a plea. I didn't listen to him. I was thinking, of vast empty spaces filled with oily, glistening bubbles. They popped and spawned yet more bubbles, then more still until they filled everything with rainbow color, expanding through the solar system, the quadrant, the galaxy and out, never stopping, into the infinite blackness beyond, engulfing everything in their path and humming along as they ravaged.

"Shut it off," I said. "Do it now, before it's too late."

He looked at me as if I was insane.

"But we've done it, Duncan. This is 'fortune and glory' stuff, right here; this is our place in the history books."

"Bugger the books. I'll just be happy to have some more history. Shut it down."

He finally turned to the contraption. This time I was looking at the egg as he tried to manage the shutdown.

It was indeed too late.

Two eggs now hung on the shelf side by side, just touching, each as black as the other, twin bubbles of space-time only held in check by Muir's incomprehensible *boundary field*. I was suddenly all too aware how fragile that field had been the day before. The hum throbbed louder. The eggs pulsed in synchronized agreement.

"Do something, Muir."

"I'm trying," he said, pulling out copper wire and untwisting valves to no apparent effect. The throb from the field went up a notch until it felt like being inside a vast kettledrum beaten by a manic giant.

This time it was Muir who didn't see, but I saw only too well. The valves screamed in the hurt of overexertion; the lights flickered, threatened to go out completely. I couldn't take my eyes off the eggs. An area of misty fog coalesced around them, spreading over the dark eggs. Two things happened almost simultaneously, and even later I wasn't sure which came first; Muir shouted "I've got it," and fog *breathed* then winked out of existence. The black eggs went with it.

The remaining valves whined. The noise of their effort faded back down to the almost comforting drone I was more accustomed to. Muir looked up, his fear and excitement vying for supremacy. In him, the excitement seemed to be winning—not so much in my case.

"That's it. We're done," I said, and went in search of a smoke. The hybrid beast in the tank slithered and beat its claw excitedly against the glass tank as I left.

Muir came out onto the porch seconds after I'd got a smoke lit. He took the cigarette from me, sucked down a deep one, then flicked the butt away with his forefinger and thumb. We didn't speak—I had no idea what I was going to say, but Muir had questions of his own for me.

"You saw it this time, didn't you?"

"The fog? Yes, I saw it."

"*The fog?* Yes, that's about right. I thought it was more smoke-like myself, but I'll go with *fog*." He laughed.

"This is no joking matter, Muir. What the hell just happened?"

"*Hell* might be an appropriate word," he replied. "There are stories in many cultures of precisely this kind of phenomenon; they tell of a supernatural beast that controls the gateways—of perception—of reality—call it what you will. The dweller on the threshold—you might have heard of it?"

"You've lost me, old man."

"Think of it this way. Suppose there's a natural protective mechanism in the fabric of each universe, something that stops one bleeding into another—a unifying force ensuring that the glue sticks the whole thing together without the bubbles bursting?"

"And you think that's what I saw?"

He nodded.

"And if I'm right, we can keep experimenting. If we make a mistake, your fog will stop us from doing any real damage."

I saw in his eyes that he was deadly serious.

"No, Muir. I said it, and I meant it, I'm done here."

I thought he might plead with me, even beg, but he just went quiet—in a way, that was much worse.

I stuck to my guns for most of the afternoon. I sat in the shade of the porch, sipping beer and smoking a pipe while Muir huffed and puffed, got sweaty and swore a lot, attempting to transfer his new supplies over to the shed. Several of the locals joined me in watching the sport, but no one raised a hand to help and Muir was getting rather tetchy by the time he had everything transported and stowed to his liking.

He didn't even look at me as he went into the shed and closed the door firmly enough for a waft of dust and splinters to fall lazily to the ground from its surface.

After that there was nothing to see—but plenty to hear as the garden filled with sounds of sawing and hammering, then more sinisterly a rising hum and vibration. Blue light flashed, brighter than the sun—it seemed Muir had succeeded in hooking up his new battery.

"I'm warning you," the innkeeper said at my back. "I'll be over there with my shotgun at the first sign of anything hinky."

Hinky was the least of my worries—I was thinking again of those hanging eggs, the fog that had enveloped them, and Muir's attempt at an explanation. One universe was just fine for me—I didn't need to get close to any more.

I had thought I would be content to stick with my resolution to leave Muir to it, but the rising hum had become insistent, the blue flashes more frequent and the overall sense that *something* was about to happen was almost palpable. I could not in all honesty leave my countryman to face a possible imminent danger all alone. With more bravado than I felt, I knocked out the pipe, downed the last dregs of the beer, and went to watch Muir play God.

He had indeed made his contraption larger—it now filled the whole long shelf in the shed, wood and corrugated iron, valves and batteries all connected with many yards of copper wire, all blue haze, all dancing.

The vibration was loud even above the high whining of the valves. I saw why as soon as I looked up above the shelf.

Four eggs hung in a tight group, pulsing in time with the magnetic throb. Colors danced and flowed across the sheer black surface; blues and greens and shimmering silvers that were now all too familiar.

"Shut that bloody thing off," I shouted. Muir ignored me. All his attention was on those four eggs—four universes, if he was to be believed, maybe even infinite in their own way. The enormity of what we were doing had finally hit me, and I was struck immobile, only able to look on as each of the eggs trembled and calved.

In the blink of an eye there were eight.

The crystal valves howled in anguish. I was vaguely aware of Muir attempting to connect yet another battery to the system, but I was past caring, lost in contemplation of the beauty in front of me.

Sixteen now, all perfect, all dancing.

"We need more juice," Muir shouted, as he connected the new battery into the series. The hum went up another level. The eggs calved again.

Thirty-two now, and they had started to fill the shed with dancing aurora of shimmering lights that pulsed and capered in time with the vibration and the whine of the valves, everything careening along in a big happy dance.

"Duncan!" Muir shouted. "I need you."

I kept ignoring him.

Sixty-four, each a shimmering pearl of black light.

The colors filled the shed, spilled out across the shelf, crept among the sample jars, danced in my eyes, in my head, all through my body. I gave myself to it, willingly.

And I would be gone yet if I hadn't felt a flicker of memory.

It only came when it was needed the most.

I managed to turn toward Muir.

"Shut it down," I said. "That's what's causing the problem."

Once again, he looked at me as if I was insane.

"The *gatekeeper* will come when we most need it," I said, having to shout to be heard above the growing din. "The *Dweller* is the glue—let it come. It will hold everything together—it will stop these universes expanding into ours."

I saw comprehension hit him. He pulled all the wires out from the where they were attached to the batteries. The drone faded to a whisper, the drumbeat slowing and diminishing, leaving us in almost complete silence.

A hundred and twenty-eight now, and already calving into two-hundred and fifty-six. The shed was filling fast.

The structure shook and quaked, fine dust falling all around us.

"Something's happening," Muir whispered.

It started with a flicker in the corner of the shed, but grew and thickened and spread until a glowing fog enfolded what I guessed to be a thousand and twenty-four eggs. A crack ran through the wall to my left, and two of the sample jars on the far side of the shed toppled with a crash.

The hybrid. I forgot about the hybrid.

I looked down to the long glass tank. The beast was still there, slithering and squirming. The four beady eyes were watching the calving of the eggs with what looked to me like anticipation.

The fog breathed in, breathed out, twice. There was a sudden burst of color; red, blue and shimmering silver filled my head.

I blinked, looked back, and the eggs were gone as quickly as they had come—there was only the empty containment chamber. But the damage had been done. The crack in the wall widened. A portion of the roof collapsed, fell to the floor and immediately disintegrated into dust. Muir and I looked at each other, then made for the door.

We only just made it in time. The whole shed was coming down around us. We burst through the door together, reducing it completely to dust and splinters in the process. We emerged into sunlight, blinking, as the shed caved in on itself at our back.

A pall of dust rose up from the ruined building, and was taken away by the wind. I might have been the only one that noticed, but before it dispersed it seemed to thicken and lighten, almost glowing. A thick fog hung above the garden for a long second, breathed, twice, then it was gone.

The locals burned what was left of the shed, much to Muir's disgust, but I could hardly blame them after they got a look at the writhing thing that crawled in the ruins of the fish tank. Once it had raised that huge claw and clacked it in the innkeeper's direction, its fate was sealed. And I don't care what universe you come from—a double-barreled shotgun at close range is going to slow you down a tad.

They burned everything—samples, batteries, valves and wood. The fire burned until after sundown, and I watched it closely—there may have been a hint of a rainbow aura—but only a hint, and there was no recurrence of the fog.

I had the innkeeper sell me a bottle of Scotch and I returned to my room, where I have been writing this memoir while making what I see are serious inroads on the contents of said bottle. Muir has been at the door twice but I do not wish to speak to him now—maybe not for a long time to come.

This time, I really am done with this place.

13

Present Day

I don't remember much about the short drive on the Skidoo back to the depot. At least the wind was mostly at my back and kept the snow out of my face—my instincts did the rest, keeping me on the right track and stopping me from collapsing into a quivering heap of misery by the roadside.

Old Pat took one look at me when I entered the depot and went straight for the booze again, pouring me a large measure in a coffee mug.

"That bad?" he asked as I downed the contents in one gulp that did a lot to put fire back in my belly.

"Worse," I replied, and he must have seen it in my eyes, for he didn't press me.

George looked up from where he was sitting by the radio set.

"The good news is that it's been quiet here," he said. "The bad news is it's been quiet here. We don't have any idea if everybody's okay or if they're..."

He didn't continue—he didn't have to, we all knew what he meant.

Pat offered me more liquor but I shook my head, despite it shouting loud at me.

"I need to get back out there," I said. "I need to check on folks."

"And what will you do?" Pat said softly. "What can you do?"

I had no answer to that—all I knew was that I couldn't just sit on my hind end and wait. I checked the clock, and was surprised to find it was nearly five in the morning.

"It'll be light in a couple of hours," I said. "I don't think it's ever been seen in daylight, has it?"

"Son," Pat replied. "With that fucker, I don't think we can take anything for granted."

"What the hell have we done to deserve this?" I said. It was meant to be a rhetorical question, but old Pat took it seriously.

"There's no rhyme or reason to it, lad—there never has been over the years. But it has never taken folks like this before—something must have changed. I suspect somebody's going to have to go over to the wreck at some point soon and see what's what. I vote it's not me."

I had a smoke before I headed back out to the Skidoo—I had to clear a couple of inches of fresh snow from the saddle before climbing on—the storm wasn't showing signs of slowing down anytime soon. Pat and George stood in the doorway, looking as glum as if they were at my funeral.

"I'll do a quick turn round the town," I shouted. "Back in twenty."

They looked as if they believed it almost as much as I did.

I kicked the sled into gear and pulled out of the depot into the white hell that waited.

I've said before, I love the solitude of being out on the road during a storm—but that was when I was in the relative warmth of the cabin of the plow. Things were a bit different on the Skidoo—the weather blew raw in my face, wind buffeting and pushing, threatening at any moment to discard me by the roadside. Despite extra padding and gloves, I still felt cold bite deep in my bones. Even twenty minutes out in these conditions was going to be pushing it.

The town was quiet, despite the storm raging through it, as if waiting in anticipation for what might get thrown at it next. I saw no signs of life on the short portion of the trip that took me first to the church hall.

Nobody else had turned up since my last visit, and I didn't hang around—it reminded me too much that everyone who had been here so short a time ago was now gone. I promised myself that the fog wouldn't take another soul that night—although I had no idea how I was going to keep it.

I turned away from the church and went down into town, riding the drifts as if they were waves. I passed the bank and went down the slope toward the theater on the old dockside, knowing that they had an overhung carport where I might at least get some respite from the wind.

It was not to be. At first, I thought that the blowing snow had obscured my sight, but as I closed in there was no doubt about it—the theater was gone. Where it had stood was just another area of melted and hardened material—wood, glass, roof slate and piping all welded hard together. The saving grace was that the place would have been empty of people—but the largest building in town had gone completely—and without anybody noticing.

How much more of my town had gone the same way?

I almost lost control of the sled on the steep incline down to the car park that led onto the old quayside—but I had to go and check down there—I needed to know just how much of our history was being stripped from us.

At least the post office was still intact, although there was no sign of life there either, which gave me pause for thought—old Mrs. Malloy liked to keep the place open on stormy nights, dispensing coffee and a shoulder to cry on for anyone who needed it. She'd been my teacher back in the day, her foghorn voice doing much to keep unruly kids in line during days when the sun called louder than lessons. She hadn't been among the crowd who headed out from the church hall—I'd have heard her if she'd been there. It looked like I had someone else to go and check on.

First, I went all the way down to the end of the quay. The old town hall to my right and the gift shop and coffee bar at the far end of the quay were reassuring, looming shadows on the trip down—the fog hadn't taken them.

Not yet, a voice whispered in my head, but I pushed it away—that was something I'd been thinking about all too often later—if I survived the night. I didn't need it in my head now.

I stopped on the quayside under the coffee bar's porch, sheltered from the elements by the bulk of the bar itself and the fact it was down in a hollow on the shore. I was closer to the water than I'd liked, but at least I'd see anything coming from that direction. I shut off the engine and sat there, listening to the storm whistle and rage. The sea in the old harbor danced in a frenzy with the wind, lashed by sheets of snow that caught in eddy points among the cliffs to the east and swirled like dervishes.

It was all strangely beautiful, but I knew only too well how deadly it could be to get lost in its charms. I thought about having a smoke, but I had no time to waste. I kicked the sled into gear and headed back off the quay and off along the shore road, once again heading toward the old part of town on the peninsula.

If anything, it was even quieter down here. The streetlights were few and far between, and the houses sat back off the road in larger gardens. There had been no plowing since my run-through earlier, and the snow was piled high—six-foot drifts and more in places. I saw no sign of life until I got to the old

Village Inn. Someone had tried to leave—and they hadn't made it. I saw the remains of at least three bodies on the ground outside the main door—they had been caught, like flies on sticky paper, caught and stretched and violated until there were barely recognizable as human at all. The snow was stained red around where they lay—I didn't go too close. There was little point in checking for life signs in bodies that had been so brutally torn and abused.

I realized as I turned away that my fear had gone, all drained away by too much repetition, too much exposure to the horror. It was anger I felt now, a rage that was getting stronger by the second—I needed a reckoning. Something was going to pay for what it had done—what it was still doing—to my town.

Old Mrs. Malloy's place was one of the most exposed properties on the peninsula, perched high on an outcrop looking straight out over the expanse of the bay. I almost didn't make it up the road that led to the property—the outcrop was exposed to the full brunt of the storm. Wind tore at my clothing, tugging and pushing and rocking the Skidoo violently from side to side. The only saving grace was that the snow wasn't drifting up here, but was getting blown straight off without being allowed a purchase. I brought the sled to a halt on an almost clear patch by the old lady's front porch.

The house was an older property—no vinyl siding here, just good sturdy wood. It had stood up to worse storms than this one and I fervently hoped it would see many more to come. There was a light on above the main door. That gave me hope. I leaned heavily on the doorbell, unable to hear if it was working above the howl of the wind.

No one came.

I bent and peered through the letterbox.

"Mrs. Malloy? Are you okay?"

This time it wasn't anything I wanted to hear—it was muffled, and at first I wasn't certain that it wasn't just the wind whistling, then it came again, and I was sure—it was a woman—Mrs. Malloy. She was wailing for help as loud as she'd ever berated any schoolboy. I put my good shoulder into the door and knocked it off its hinges as I went to her aid.

I'd been wrong about the old house standing up to anything that was thrown at it. As at the Connors earlier, the damage had been done at the rear of the house, where the screaming was coming from. I followed the noise. The back wall of the kitchen had flowed and collapsed before hardening—I'd seen something similar in a poster on a student's bedroom wall way back when—some Spanish artist. This looked similar—but I don't think Mrs. Malloy ever modeled for Dalí.

She had become intimately acquainted with her refrigerator—her lower body from the hips down was encased in stainless steel, plastic, milk cartons and food containers, all fused and amalgamated with ruined flesh. The floor was awash with orange juice, broken eggs and blood.

But the old lady was still very much alive, and still screaming. She didn't stop when she saw me in the doorway.

"Help me," she yelled. "Please, help me."

I walked gingerly over to the fused mess. I didn't want to look—but I had to, just to check if my suspicions were true. Unfortunately, they were—the only way Mrs. Malloy was going to be moved was if we took the full refrigerator with her. I honestly did not know how she could possibly still be alive without having gone completely mad—she was obviously made of stern stuff.

And she proved it by grabbing my hand, tight.

"Well, Francis," she said, using my Sunday name that only she and my mum ever called me by. "If you're not going to get me out of this fucking fridge, you could at least get me a smoke and a drink."

The incongruity of sitting on a chair in a devastated kitchen handing a cigarette and a full glass of vodka to a woman embedded in a fridge was not lost on either of us.

Mrs. Malloy tried to laugh but had to stop when she brought up blood.

"This is another fine mess you've gotten me into," she said, sucked on the smoke and coughed again, spattering blood among the spilled eggs and juice. "These things are going to kill me one of these days."

"Don't talk," I said, and that got another laugh.

"What, and break the habit of a lifetime?" She downed the vodka in one. "I'm going to need more, Francis. I don't think I need to worry about getting drunk, do you?"

I poured her another full glass. She made short work of it.

"Well, at least I'll go with a smile on my face now," she said.

"We should try something…" I started before she interrupted.

"I'm done trying, Francis. I've been screaming my head off and squirming like a scalded cat for an hour—I'm done. Just stay with me—it won't be long now. Tell me how things are out there."

I took her hand, but I didn't tell her what I'd seen that night—she didn't need that hurt, she had enough of her own to deal with. She wasn't so far gone that she didn't know I was lying when I told her things weren't too bad, but she didn't push it. I guess, at the end, she was indeed done.

I was still holding her hand when she finally passed.

I went out to the Skidoo, having to wipe tears from my eyes before I noticed that the sky had lightened somewhat.

Dawn was coming.

14

From the journal of Duncan Campbell, 24th July 1955

Third time's a charm, or so they say.

I was all packed and ready to go this morning, determined that I was indeed done with Muir and his experiments. If I'd been awake ten minutes earlier and slipped out then, I might be well on my way back home by now. Instead, I'm still here, in the room at the Village Inn, scribbling away in this journal in the hope I might make some sense of what has happened and what we must do tomorrow.

As I have said, I did not manage to slip out. Muir banged on my door again, just past six thirty this morning. I opened the door, fully intending to walk past him and down the stairs. That was until I looked in his eyes.

"For pity's sake, man, what is the matter now?"

He herded me back into the room and closed the door, as if worried that someone might see.

"You can't go, Duncan," he said.

"Give me one good reason not to," I replied.

"I need you," he said quietly.

"You need your head examined, that's what you need," I said.

He sat down heavily on the edge of the bed and undid the cuff of his shirt.

"No, I really need you," he said. He rolled up his sleeve. The arm he exposed wasn't just an arm. "I guess we didn't get out of that shed fast enough."

I saw tendons and flesh through a hand-sized piece of glass that seemed to have taken the place of his skin along the inside of his forearm. It looked almost opaque, and grooved, as if it had melted then reformed. There was a soft, translucent appearance to the flesh beneath the glass that I did not like the look of at all.

"And there's these," he said, lifting his shirt up to expose his midriff. A double row of penny-sized octopus-like suckers ran in long columns from his nipples down to his navel, red and moist, like obscene mouths. He lowered his shirt quickly, as if embarrassed, but it would never hide the memory of it, which I feared was now seared in my brain forever more. It took me several seconds to notice that Muir was still talking.

"I need to get back out to that wreck, Duncan. I need to bring up my original kit from down there—or as much as can be salvaged anyway—and figure out what we did wrong last year—it's the only chance I've got of reversing the bally thing. Remember how we kept the phenomenon at bay for a while at the end there on the deck? That's part of what we need to do now. I need to stabilize the field, then reverse its effects—and we should be quick about it."

I had scarcely heard him, my mind still full of the sight of those wet suckers, pulsing in time with his breathing, every bit as much part of him as his eyes or his fingers.

How is such a thing even possible?

"Duncan?" he said, softly, almost a whimper. "Please? You're the only one who understands."

I was very far from understanding, but Muir was in so much pain—emotional even more so than physical—that I could not refuse him. Within the hour we were back in the creel boat, heading once more for Dunfield Bay and the wreck site.

The weather had taken a turn for the worse. Fine cold drizzle accompanied us all the way out of the bay and along the shore toward the Tern Rock and beyond. Even Indian Head Rock seemed morose and sullen as we passed it.

We had the sea mostly to ourselves apart from some gulls overhead and a pod of boisterous porpoises some distance to the east of us. I chain-smoked cigarettes while Muir took the wheel, and I tried not to think too much of the glass panel in his arm, or the wet suckers at his belly. Thankfully he kept his shirt on during the trip, and when we eventually arrived above the wreck, I averted my eyes as he stripped down to his trunks, snorkel and mask combination. He dropped a long, thin rope over the side, tying it on to the hull.

"I'll tug twice if there's something to bring up," he said, and I nodded.

"Be careful," I replied. "And be quick. If anything swims up that isn't you, I'll be off and away before you can say 'Jack Robinson'."

"I'm taking precautions," Muir replied. "I've got this."

I had to turn toward him to see what he meant. He had a knife strapped to his ankle—but that wasn't what drew my gaze. I couldn't help but stare at his arm. The flesh beneath the glass panel didn't look like sinew and muscle much anymore—it seemed somehow thinner, more fluid, and got me thinking of the amorphous tissue in the guts of the first fish samples we had taken.

Muir saw me looking, and must have seen the worry in my gaze.

"Whatever is happening, the effect seems to be accelerating. We need to work quick, Duncan," he said, rather sharply. I dragged my gaze from the arm—the suckers, though grotesque, did not frighten me nearly so much as what I'd seen beneath that glass panel. But I steadied myself, and gave Muir a mock salute.

"Aye, aye, Cap'n," I replied, and with a smile he went over the side and down to the depths.

The quiet sea no longer felt like a tranquil place to be—I lit a fresh smoke from the butt of the last, and stood there looking down into the dark waters. With the sun behind clouds and a light breeze disturbing the water, there was no way to see into the depths, no way to know what Muir might be up to. The rope hung straight, stiff and unmoving where it hung off the hull, and no matter how much I willed it to move, it stayed resolutely still. Time passed—too much time. Muir didn't come up for air and the sea refused to give up its secrets.

I had almost finished the cigarette when the surface finally broke with a soft splash. Muir bobbed up some ten feet way, sucked gratefully on fresh air, then gave me the thumbs-up.

"I found it. It's almost all still there, Duncan," he said. "I had to hack away a bit at some kelp—but it's kept remarkably well—it must be the cold water. There will be stuff to haul up any minute now."

And with that he dived again—but not before I'd caught fresh sight of the suckers on his belly—a deeper red now, larger and pulsing, eagerly, as if taking in strength from their time in the water.

I almost jumped a foot a minute later when the rope tugged hard, twice, at the hull, rocking the boat rather violently. I bent and started to haul it up—whatever Muir had tied on down there, it was heavy, and seemed most reluctant to come back to the surface. It took almost all my energy to drag it from the depths, and by the time I could see it just below the surface, my hands were numb, cold and raw from the friction of the wet rope. Thankfully Muir came up with it, and between the two of us we were able to heave a slimy mass of chrome, metal and wiring up on deck.

Muir looked like the cat that had got the cream.

"That's most of it—back in a jiffy," he said, and went down again.

If Muir thought the stuff was remarkably well preserved, I'd have hated to see anything he considered ruined. To me it looked like a pile of partially rusted, weed-covered junk of little more use than a long-discarded bicycle—which, in truth, it rather resembled. I bent to part a thicker piece of weed to get a closer look. Something scuttled away and off over the hull to go back into the water with a soft plop. I didn't get too close a look at it, but I was sure I saw a pincer—and tentacles. It reminded me all too clearly of the strange octopus hybrid Muir had kept in the shed. If there were more of those things in the depths, I was even more resolved than ever that Muir was not going to get me to go into the water.

The rope tugged at the hull, and once again I was forced to haul. Thankfully it was a far lighter load this time, and I was able to bring it up with relative ease, although my poor hands felt more raw and sore by the time I dragged a mess of coils and wiring aboard to dump it alongside the other material already there.

The deck had become rather cramped, with all the coils, chrome and cabling. I did not see how Muir could possibly know what it all was, but when he dragged himself aboard, he pronounced himself happy with the haul.

"It's all here, Duncan," he said. "At least enough of it to make it work. I can hook it up to the boat's battery—there'll be enough juice to provide a stable field. Then it's going to be a matter of trying to find the proper vibratory matrix that will dampen the field boundary oscillation and let me either reverse—or at least halt—the physical changes that it has wrought."

Of course, that all sounded like gobbledygook to me—and on top of that, Muir was talking about the grotesque changes in his body as if they were no more than a scientific curiosity to be studied. I did not—could not—share his detachment, for the physical changes he so casually dismissed were right before my eyes. He still had not put on a shirt, and the suckers looked larger now, red and glistening with water droplets—moist, more like wet mouths than ever.

Muir saw me looking.

"Cover that up, would you, there's a good chap," I said.

He did as he was asked quickly enough, but not before I had another look through the glass panel embedded in his arm. Whatever was inside there now, it was not human—and it was not flesh. It danced and writhed in a mass of the now-familiar rainbow colors. I did not get a close enough look at it to be sure, but far from resembling blood, bone and tissue, there seemed to be nothing in there but dry, swirling dust and ash.

I took the wheel on the way back to Trinity—Muir was too busy inspecting and cleaning—or attempting to clean—the stuff he'd brought up from the wreck.

As I smoked another of what were already too many cigarettes, I remembered the scuttling thing that had escaped back over the hull.

"So, if this stuff was still down there and retrievable—did you see anything else?"

I had started by thinking about tentacles and claws—but was also thinking of the men we'd lost that night—and now I felt as if we'd just desecrated a war grave.

"There's no bodies if that's what you mean," Muir said, as if guessing my thoughts. "There are a lot of those deformed fish—and more of the wee crabby octopus things feeding on them—but everything seems to stay close to the wreck, as if there is indeed some kind of boundary field that they have to remain inside to be viable life forms."

He looked up with a thin smile on his face.

"That is only a theory, of course—but one which we may now have the ability to test."

My mind was full of random images—red wet suckers, clacking claws and slithering tentacles, but most of all the dry, gray ash and dust that swirled and danced behind the glass in Muir's forearm. I had a bad feeling in my gut. I was nowhere near as confident of a positive outcome as Muir seemed to be.

The pod of porpoises were still far offshore to starboard as we neared the entrance to Trinity harbor, tracking north and east at the same speed as us. They kept their distance, and when we turned to port to enter the sheltered waters around town, the porpoises turned east, heading out to sea. It might only have been my imagination, but they seemed somewhat sluggish, somehow lacking in the exuberance and joy they normally displayed.

My mood was somber as we tied up at the short wooden dock below the old church. I had expected Muir to insist we lug the retrieved kit back to the inn, but he showed no signs of asking me. Instead he fetched a canvas sheet from the hold and covered up what we'd brought up from the wreck.

"We'll leave this here. I don't think the locals are too keen on me at the moment," Muir said.

"That's an understatement," I replied, and got a rare smile.

"Perhaps it's best if we do this away from prying eyes?" he continued. "There's a few bits and bobs I'll need—that shouldn't be a problem. I'll meet you back in the inn for a spot of lunch, then we can get to it this afternoon?"

He must have seen my hesitation.

"Please, Duncan," he said, and the tremor was back in his voice. "I have no one else to turn to—and I fear my time is short."

He showed me his arm again—the ash-like material inside seethed and roiled against the glass. It looked thinner now.

It looked like fog.

I resisted the temptation to accompany my lunch of bread, ham and cheese with a decent snifter of rum, but I did allow myself a cold beer, the taste of which did much to ameliorate my growing gloom.

The innkeeper asked if we'd had a good trip. I could not tell him the true purpose of it, and I could not bring myself to lie to him. He had shown me not just hospitality, but also a degree of friendship that had done much to ensure my memories of this stay would not all consist of strangeness and bad science. I grunted something that I hoped sounded positive, and that seemed to satisfy him.

Muir joined me several minutes later, and our host pointedly stayed away from the table after taking his order. If Muir felt slighted, he showed no sign of it. He had regained a modicum of his old swagger.

"I've got everything we'll need," he said in a conspiratorial whisper, then we kept the conversation light and inconsequential through the rest of our admittedly excellent luncheon.

It was only when we were left alone in the small dining room that Muir started to speak about his plans for the rest of the day, but once again they were wreathed in so much science and esoteric theories that I had great difficulty following his train of thought. I will not even attempt to transcribe it here—he was thinking and speaking at the same time, sparking off new ideas and discarding them almost as quickly as they came. I do believe that if we'd had a blackboard available, he would have been scribbling notes and formulae, only to wipe them off and start again every few minutes. It was all rather exhilarating in a way—until he pushed back his shirt from his forearm, and I got another look at what was happening to him.

The glass had turned opaque, obscuring the view of the internal structure of the arm—but the melted and fused area seemed to be spreading. It covered most of the lower arm, as far up as I could see—for all I knew his whole arm was now in the same condition. That wasn't the worst thing though—when I looked down, I saw his shirt move at the belly, as if something was squirming underneath—the suckers were hungry again.

By all rights I should have trusted my instincts and fled right there and then—but Muir needed me—and he also needed someone to temper his excesses should he come to be on the verge of doing something even more monumentally stupid. After we both had another smoke, I followed him outside and down to the small jetty.

There was more stuff littering the deck of our boat now—tent poles, rigging, a toolbox and more crystal valves. I did not ask where he had procured the items in such a small town—I was past the need for explanations and just wanted to get the day over with so that I could return to the comfort of my room and lose myself in liquor.

"Well we can't do anything here in plain sight of town," Muir said. "And I'm not ready yet to go back to the wreck. What say you to mooring off Indian Head Rock? He can watch over us and keep us on the straight and narrow."

I could have made a quip about us needing all the help we could get, but held my tongue. I'd decided on my role for the rest of the day—I was going to watch Muir and make sure he didn't get anybody—including me—killed. That, and giving my attention to piloting the boat, was just about all the thinking I intended to do.

Muir busied himself in continuing to clean up the mess we had brought up from the wreck. I had my back to him for a good while as I concentrated firstly on getting the creel boat out of the harbor, then steering it across a rather stiff tide to moor off the tall Indian Head Rock. A bald eagle—possibly even the same one I'd spotted on a previous trip—sat on top of it, eyeing us warily.

I turned back to see that Muir had erected a makeshift rain cover tent across the rear deck, and had one of his contraptions assembled underneath it. The coils and wire looked rusty, and green with algae in many places, with shiny new crystal valves only making the other parts look less than capable of the job they were going to be asked to perform.

"Almost ready," Muir said. "Cut the engine, there's a good chap. I'm going to need the battery."

I was starting to see a possible flaw in Muir's planning, but I did as he asked. I cut the engine, and between us we managed to wriggle and squirm in the tight hold to get a cable attached to the battery terminals, which was then to be connected to Muir's contraption.

"Are you ready?" Muir asked.

I was about as far from ready as a man could be, but I gritted my teeth, nodded, and Muir connected the cable from the battery to a terminal on his machine.

A hum started up immediately—and the bald eagle had already seen enough. It took off from the top of the rock, leaving a squirt of guano for us to show its disdain. The hum got louder—the air tingled, like frost on the face on winter mornings, and I felt light, as if a stiff breeze might lift me up and carry me away.

"It's working," Muir shouted, but he sounded faint and distant although he stood only three feet away. A sudden swell lifted the boat and plunged us, headlong toward Indian Head Rock—and of course, we had no engine power available to do anything about it. I braced myself for impact as we looked to be smashed against the stone—I even put out a hand in the vain hope I might steady myself. Impact was imminent.

My hand met only cold air. There was a sudden feeling of heaviness—extreme weight as if stone had been laid on my chest and was pressing me inside it, like meat in a rock sandwich. For several seconds I struggled for breath, but it lifted as quickly as it had come, and the light, tingling feeling returned.

We had open water around us—and Indian Head Rock was at our backs.

The only way that was possible—an almost impossible thought in itself—was if we had just passed right through the bally thing.

Muir was beaming from ear to ear.

"It works," he shouted. "It bloody well works."

The remainder of the afternoon was taken up with a series of experiments in the waters around Indian Head Rock. The most disconcerting of them involved us taking the boat as close to the rock as we could manage, and Muir seemingly pushing his hand—and eventually his whole body—into the stone as if it were no more than some kind of projected image he could walk through.

When I asked for an explanation, his reply left me none the wiser, full as it was of talk of harmonics and magnetic resonance, words that meant little to me.

All I know is that Muir now believes we have a chance to both reverse the changes that are happening in his body and to put a stop to any lingering aftereffects of last year's experiment on the wrecked navy boat beneath the waters of Dunfield Bay.

I do hope he is right, for as we were heading back to Trinity, Muir bent over his mechanism to fiddle with a valve and I caught a glimpse of the side of his neck. Three red gouges in his skin opened and closed in time with his breathing.

If I did not know any better, I'd have said they were gill slits.

15

Present Day

The fact that dawn was coming did not improve my situation any—in fact, it made things worse, for at least I could see the glowing fog coming in the dark. Now it would just be a slightly grayer patch amid a white hell of snow, wind and more snow. The storm wasn't showing signs of abating—if anything, the snow was still getting heavier, and much of the stuff that had already fallen was getting blown around in the wind in a blinding whiteout blizzard.

I stood outside the Malloy house for several seconds, trying to decide on a course of action, and coming up with nothing. I felt powerless in the face of the thing that had gripped the town. I needed something to fight, something tangible, something real, and I was starting to fear for my sanity.

I got on the Skidoo, intending to complete my circuit of the town, but I couldn't get any farther along the peninsula—the wind was just too strong, and even with the goggles on I couldn't see beyond the front of the sled. I gave in to the inevitable and turned around, almost getting tumbled over in the process as a gust hit me sideward and reminded me just how tired I was getting as I struggled to keep the sled upright. Finally, I had her pointing in the right direction and kicked her into gear, half-driving, half-getting blown back down the slope to the oldest part of town.

I meant to head back to the depot, but as I passed the Village Inn, something seemed to shift off to my left, behind the inn itself, a darker shadow in the swirling white. I pulled the Skidoo over against the north wall where I could be sheltered slightly from the main blow of the wind, and peered into the garden area.

There was definitely something in there, although I couldn't make out any detail at this distance. Blue light flashed twice.

An electrical short?

If a line was down, I had to go and check—Dick from the hydro board wasn't going to be along to fix it. I switched off the Skidoo, made sure I was still wrapped up well against the elements, put my shoulder to the wind and headed into the Village Inn's back garden.

There were more blue flashes as I got to the corner of the house—to get any closer would mean exposing myself to the full brunt of the wind, and I wasn't about to do that unless absolutely necessary. I took a step forward.

My flesh tingled, felt almost warm.

It's the fog.

The wind dropped completely, and suddenly I was too hot, standing in a green garden under a blue sky with sunlight blazing. Another blue bolt, like a camera's flash, hit me. It came from a ramshackle shed in the center of the garden, one that seemed to be bathed in a dancing rainbow shimmer of color. Before I even had time to wonder if I had indeed lost my sanity, there was another flash. Cold wind hit me, snow spattering against my goggles. I stumbled, almost fell, and stepped back into the shelter of the old inn's north wall.

I stood there, leaning on the side of the house, breathing heavily, and waiting to see what happened next.

Nothing did, apart from more snow and more wind.

That was it for me—I'd had as much high strangeness as one man could take. I got back on the Skidoo, kicked her into life, and headed for the depot as fast as I could. I almost didn't make it up the incline to the main road, having to go full throttle to get over a huge drift, and I had a bad moment when the wind almost caught me again—but two minutes later I walked into the main room. Pat and George turned from where they sat around the stove, eyes wide as if they'd seen a ghost.

"We thought we'd lost you, boy," George said as I went to sit near the stove. "You've been gone for hours."

I brought them up to speed on what I'd seen on my trip around town. They went quiet when I told them about the theater, and even quieter when I detailed the last minutes of Mrs. Malloy's life. She'd been well-liked, especially among the older generation, and her passing was going to leave a big hole in the life of the town—if there was to be any life left in it after this storm.

I debated whether to tell them about the Village Inn garden—in a night of weirdness, it had been perhaps the weirdest thing of all, and I still wasn't too sure that I hadn't imagined it all due to stress. Pat looked about to speak, but just then the radio beeped for an incoming call. George took it—I was too tired to do much beyond sit still and soak up heat.

George nodded his head a lot and looked solemn as he answered the call.

"We'll be waiting, I hope," he said. "Over." He turned away from the radio, and kept us in suspense by lighting a smoke before telling us. "That was the government boys we've been expecting. They're at Irving Station—they say half an hour—I said two. Somewhere in between is probably a good enough guess. Chin up, Frank—we'll get through this."

"It's not me I'm worried about," I replied.

Pat passed me a smoke.

"There's little more you can do, lad," he said. "You've done more than anyone would have asked of you on a night like this. Besides—I've got a story you might need to hear—if you've got that itch out of your hind-end and can sit still for its telling?"

I took the smoke and sucked gratefully.

"I'm going nowhere until the cavalry gets here," I replied. "Just let George fetch us some coffee and the floor is yours."

We finished the smokes while George fetched the coffee. With the wind still raging outside, Pat took us back to a summer's night, some years before I was born.

16

1969

"It weren't long after Neil Armstrong walked on the moon," Pat started. "And I'll tell you how I was reminded of that later—but best if I start at the beginning. It'll make more sense that way.

"I wasn't in town for the kerfuffle in the fifties—I was away in the Navy, seeing the world and having a rare old time. But by the late Sixties I'd got all that out of my system and had settled down in a house along the shore—just past the Malloy place. It was a lovely spot in the summer, but a bitch to heat in the winter.

"Anyway, to cut to the chase, I did most of my drinking in the Village Inn—it wasn't exactly Bali or Cairo, but any port in a storm as they say. That July night we had a few tourists sitting in a corner, but it was mainly local lads at the bar. George's dad was sitting next to me, and your grandfather, Frank, was farther along the bar. Alan, the innkeeper, was there too. He was the only one who'd seen what happened in the fifties, but he'd told the story often enough that when young Eddie Todd came running in saying there was a weird color in the garden—well, we all had to go out and see what was what.

"I'd heard Alan's story many times—we all had—but I thought he'd added a few touches over the years to make it a better tale—that was something an old sailor knew plenty about, for I've done the same myself. But as it turned out, he had never done justice to the color at all—I certainly didn't expect it to be so beautiful.

"I've seen the aurora borealis, several times. This was like seeing it right up close—as if it were dancing, just for me, some three feet above my head. My skin was all a tingle, and the air blazed in blues and greens and gold, swathes of it, like surging waves after a storm. There was music to it too, a vibration that thrummed in my gut like a tight guitar string being continually plucked.

"The colors themselves seemed to be rising from the big bare patch in the lawn—ash and dust where the shed had been back in the day—the spot where Alan said nothing ever grew. A fine mist—not quite fog, not quite smoke, but something in between, rose up from the ground like a fountain, opening out into the spray of dancing light and music above us.

"I could have stood there watching it all night—I might well have. But the aurora hadn't been the only thing that young Eddie Todd noticed. He tugged hard at my arm, trying to get me to look at something besides the dancing lights.

"'It went under the porch,' he said. I could tell by the look in his eyes that he was scared—scared and excited at the same time, almost fit to burst with it all. I managed to tear my gaze from the lights above me and turned my attention downward.

"'What did, boy?'

"'A dog—I think,' Eddie replied. 'But not exactly, if you catch my drift.'

"I didn't, but I bent to look anyway. As I hunkered down to ground level, something shifted in the crawl space under my foot, and suddenly I wasn't so sure this was a good idea. I was thinking coyote—hungry and rabid and as likely to tear my face off as to lick my hand.

"I heard a noise, a loud snap—it was a sound I thought I recognized. At the same moment, there was another shifting below us, the whole porch moving slightly underfoot.

"Alan must have noticed that I wasn't looking up at the light show. He came down to my level.

"'You got something under there, Pat?'

I nodded.

"'Eddie says it's a dog. I'm not so sure. I thought I heard something click—like a big crab maybe? But if it is, it's the biggest fucker there's ever been.'

"I thought that might get me a laugh, but Alan went quiet, real fast. He turned to Eddie Todd.

"'Fetch me the rake, boy,' he said. 'It should be against the back door—and be quick about it.'

"While Eddie did as he was told, Alan and I sat on our haunches trying to peer under the porch. He had me spooked now, so I wasn't about to look any closer than I needed to. All I had to do was look at Alan's face to see that he thought we were in some kind of trouble, and I was old enough by then to know better than to go hunting for it.

"'What is it?' I asked, but I didn't get a reply. The others were all still staring at the light show. Nobody spoke—that's the main thing I remember. Normally you couldn't get a man of this bunch to keep quiet long enough to get a word in edgeways—but that night they were dumbstruck—a word I'd never thought to be true, but here it was, in the garden of my local bar.

"While I was musing over that, young Eddie returned with the rake—and a long billhook, one of those ones we use to bring in the codfish. He handed the rake to Alan, but kept the hook, holding it in front of his body as if expecting to have to defend himself from attack.

"Alan poked the rake under the porch. Something immediately scurried away, with several accompanying loud clacks. I knew then it weren't any kind of coyote; and it turned out to be far stranger than that. Alan moved the rake around a bit more, and seemed to get it snagged on something. The scurrying under the porch got more frantic.

"'Got you, fucker,' Alan said, and started to pull.

Now you boys know, I been all over the world, and I seen some strange sights in my time—but nothing stranger than what Alan pulled out from under the porch that night. At first sight I thought it was a bloody huge squid—it had long tentacles, and an oily, slimy body. But it was the size of a small dog—and no squid ever had eyes like that—four of them there were, on little stalks that swiveled as it looked straight at me and down into the pit of my soul. I was afraid of the thing even before I saw that huge claw—something that belonged on the biggest fucking lobster you'll ever see, and didn't look right at all on the rest of the body.

"'What the hell is that?' I asked, but Alan was in no mood for questions. He dragged the full body of the thing out from where it was still trying to scurry away and hide.

"Now that it was fully out in the open, I could see that its skin—if that was the right word for it—wasn't really oily. It was made up of the same stuff as the light show above our heads—blue and green and gold, all shifting and pulsing in time with its labored breathing.

"Nobody was looking at the lights now—all eyes were on the thing at Alan's feet.

"'Give me a hand here, lads,' Alan said, but nobody moved at first, all of us unable to quite believe what we were looking at. The thing raised its claw and clacked at us angrily. Alan tugged at the rake—he had it embedded where the ribs might be in an ordinary beast. There was no blood, no inner fluid, just puffs of rainbow dust that rose in the air each time Alan pulled.

"The innkeeper turned to young Eddie.

"'Get the spare kerosene, Eddie. Quickly, boy.'

"I took the billhook from the lad, at the same instant as the thing made a lunge, straight at Alan, that huge claw raised for attack. What I did next was pure instinct. I brought the hook up and down, hard, right into the thing's back. It fell in on itself with a soft crumpling motion, as if it was made of little more than skin and ash.

"Alan stomped down on it, hard, his heavy boot leaving an imprint behind on the ground among a body that had fallen into just a heap of dust and ash. Colored dust wafted in the air for a second, then fell to the ground. The light show flickered, blazed blue, just once, then was gone, leaving us with only the image of the light behind our eyes and sifting, crumbling dust on the ground at our feet. Alan's footprint sat in the middle of it—as clear as any left by Armstrong on the moon.

"Some of the others bent for a close look at the ash and dust, prodding and poking at it with their fingers. I'm glad now I weren't one of them, for two at least—George's dad for one—were dead within the year—cancer, they said, but do you know what I think? I think when they opened the dead men up, they might have found little more than a lot of that dancing rainbow dust.

"Alan tossed the rake aside as Eddie returned with the kerosene. We all stood back as he poured the whole can—a gallon or more—over the remains of the dead thing and set it alight. We got another light show for a few minutes—orange and yellow and blazing, although we didn't enjoy that one quite so much.

"Then we went back inside and started to get as much booze inside us as we could manage."

17

Present Day

It was only when Pat got out a smoke and lit it that I realized his story was done.

"My pa never told me any of that," George said softly.

"Weren't no reason for any of us to tell anybody," Pat replied. "Alan didn't want it broadcast around town—it wouldn't have done what little custom he got much good, would it? Besides, he was worried the thing might come back again. 'I've already burned the bloody thing twice,' he said. 'How many times will I have to do it before it stays down?'"

I was wondering how to connect what I'd seen at the inn's garden with Pat's story, but so far, I was coming up blank. All I knew was that I'd seen something—time slip, vision or mirage? Damned if I knew, or whether it made any difference, whichever it might have been. Pat seemed to have been thinking along similar lines.

"Seems like the inn is some kind of focal point for whatever is going on here, doesn't it?" Pat asked, looking at me.

I nodded.

"The inn, and over the wreck in Dunfield Bay. The fucker has its favorite places, just like regular folks do. It doesn't help us any to know though—it's not as if it hasn't been turning up in other places. And a billhook wouldn't have helped me any out at the campsite."

Nor would it have helped old Mrs. Malloy.

I sat staring at the stove—I was done, physically and mentally, completely wiped out and now running on fumes and instinct. My brain felt full of something soft and fuzzy, and I struggled to keep my eyes open for all of a minute before I gave in and fell into the blackness of dreamless sleep.

18

1856
From the journal of an unnamed seaman, discovered in Trinity Town Archives

"The Irishman's in trouble."

It was no night to be out on the water, but it was an unwritten law in Trinity. If one of us is in trouble, we all are. I drank down the shot of rum I had but left the ale where it sat. The sea was going to be rough enough as it was without having sour beer rolling in my guts as well. I was in a crowd of about a score that headed out to the dock to peer through the wind and spray.

"How far out?" someone asked.

"Out past Indian Head Rock toward Dunfield Bay. Floundering bad and holed on the port side," came the answer. "We'll need four boats at least."

The long rowboats normally took eight men each, but we had to leave room for bringing the Irishman and his crew back with us if need be. We set out, five boats with four of us in each, rowing hard into a headwind and swell that threatened to send us as far back as forward with every stroke.

It wasn't the first time I'd been out in such conditions, but it was a first attempt to rescue a big whaler such as *The Dubliner*. I knew they'd been out for three weeks, and guessed they might even have a catch aboard. Their weight, the weather, and the sheer number of crew we were going to have to shift were large in my mind as I heaved on my oar, trying to ignore the increasing pain and tiredness that I knew was only the start of the evening's trials.

By the time we reached the narrows—the outlet from the relative calm of the harbor into the rougher seas of the larger bay beyond—we were all near spent, and matters weren't helped much when the first boat out got caught in heavy swell and tipped over. They were too far away for us to help, but I saw clear enough that all four men made it to higher ground ashore, although their boat was smashed into so much kindling against the rocks below them.

The men clambered up to the point and waved that they were safe. I knew they were soaked to the skin, and had a long, wet walk ahead of them to get back to the warmth of a tavern. But I couldn't waste time worrying on their part, as we too had to fight the rising swell and a crosswind that threatened to send us to the same fate as we headed along the exposed shore.

I was so busy concentrating on keeping us upright and moving forward, that I was nearly thrown from my seat as the prow hit something, hard. I turned to yell an oath at Roberts at the bow…and looked up to see the massive bulk of *The Dubliner* loom over us.

I helped Roberts and Gallagher tie us up, and we got the other three boats alongside so that we were all arranged in a line along the whaler's keel on the starboard side, protected from the wind. It was around then I started to worry. I would have expected someone topside to have at least acknowledged our presence. Instead all we could hear was the whistling wind and the crash of waves.

"Ahoy aboard," Roberts called out. He had a bellow like a foghorn and if there were anyone aboard they'd surely hear him. But we got no answer. I saw the same fear in Gallagher's eyes that I felt. Nothing good had happened here. And I wasn't at all sure that any good was going to come of us investigating further.

But as I said already; if one is in trouble, we all are. When Roberts started to clamber out the rowboat to head up onto *The Dubliner,* I was second in line behind him, with Gallagher at my heels.

As I climbed, I steeled myself for the sights to come; I'd seen plenty of dead men smashed to no more than broken puppets by storms, and I expected that more of the same awaited us on deck.

I climbed over the gunwales and stood beside Roberts. The deck lay empty save for the large whale carcass on the platform at the stern. My fears of finding corpses were allayed, for the moment, but I had a sinking feeling in my gut as I realized we were going to have to search the vessel.

The deck lurched beneath us as the boat was caught in a larger swell, and for a second I thought we were going to be tumbled back over the side, but the keel righted itself; this time.

As the boat steadied, more men came up out of the rowboats. Roberts waited until there were more than a dozen of us on deck, then organized the search. I went with Gallagher and Roberts himself. We headed for the crew quarters, while others went to search the engine room, the mess and the cargo holds. Four men were put to work trying to get the vessel moving again, the plan being to get her at least through the narrows to quieter waters in the sheltered bay inside.

The first thing that struck me as we went below was the quiet. The big steam engine wasn't running and there was no one at the wheel as we passed. And as we went down, the silence seemed to fall on us like a blanket. Several oil lamps hung overhead at irregular intervals, and they provided a modicum of light, but as they swung in the swell, they cast bands of dark shadows along our way, shadows that seemed to cavort and caper, leading us deeper into what I feared would be our own doom.

I'm not afraid to admit that my legs felt like jelly, and every fiber of me just wanted to flee, back to the tavern and the welcoming arms of as much rum as I could get inside of me. But for the presence of Roberts and Gallagher, I might even have allowed myself to succumb to the terror. But my fear of ridicule was stronger still, and I followed Roberts as we went deeper into the boat.

The captain, Irish Frank, wasn't in his cabin. It was empty save for a bottle of rum on the sideboard that shouted at me even as we turned away to the corridor. When we looked inside the next cabin, I wished I had listened.

We had found our first corpse.

At first, I was not entirely sure what I was seeing. It looked like someone had left a pile of clothing on the floor. Then I saw the blood, a slimy trail of it that led in a six-inch-wide strip away from the clothing, across the floor…and then up the wall to where it stopped at the open porthole. As I bent for a closer look, it became all too obvious that what was left of a man was still inside the clothing. It was little more than a sack of dry skin and bones, papery, almost like ash, as if all the wet parts had been somehow sucked out of him. I heard Gallagher gag and spew, but I couldn't take my eyes off the sight. I had no idea what could do this to a man; I only knew that I did not want to meet the culprit anytime soon.

"I know that jacket," Roberts said softly. "It's Edward Malone."

I forced myself to take another look. Roberts was right. It was Ed, or rather what was left of him. A fierce drinker, a born seaman…and a man who would fight you as quick as look at you. Anything that could reduce so ferocious a sailor to a pile of rags and leave no sign of a struggle was most definitely nothing I wanted to meet. I started to back away when Gallagher shouted from out in the corridor.

"There's another one here."

Now that we knew what to look for, we found more remains at every turn. And in each case, we found no indication as to the cause of the deaths, only more bloody trails, most of which led from the bodies to outside of the vessel by the most direct route available.

"What in blazes happened here?" Gallagher whispered.

Neither Roberts nor I had an answer for him, but we wouldn't have had time in any case. The silence was broken by a scream from above; a yell of pain and suffering that tore at my heart to hear it.

We headed topside at a run.

We arrived on deck to a scene of bloody chaos. Men ran and screamed, blood flew, the wind howled and the vessel bucked and rolled beneath us. And all around, beasts slithered, too fast for the eye to follow, only being still where they had affixed themselves to some poor sailor. On first sight, I took them for octopus or squid, for they had bunches of sucker-laden tentacles that they used to cling to their prey. These tentacles were attached to a head the size of a man's clenched fist. But no octopus ever had pincers, and these most clearly did—sleek, black and as deadly as any blade as they clacked and cut and butchered any that they caught.

And no squid ever had a face like these. The eyes were the worst, four of them each, bobbing on stalks that swiveled this way and that as they searched for more prey. The stalks sat above a mouth of sorts, an elongated tube of muscular tissue that pierced the victim's butchered bodies and started to feed.

The moist sucking noises reached us even above the howling of the wind, and I do believe that sound was the most terrible aspect of the whole scene.

The beasts seemed to be everywhere, swarming across the deck in fast, fluid motion. Six men had already fallen, and three more feebly tried to keep the ravenous beasts away from them with little success. Gallagher reacted first; he jumped at the nearest beast and tried to drag it off its victim. All he succeeded in doing was tear a fist-sized lump of flesh away from the poor man's chest. The creature writhed and squirmed in Gallagher's hands, tentacles quickly circling his wrists and starting to squeeze. Its pincer clacked open and shut, looking for something to cut.

"Get the bastard thing off me," Gallagher shouted.

Roberts obliged him, but was more circumspect in his approach. He stepped quickly down below deck and came back with an oil lamp.

"Turn your head, man," he said to Gallagher, then, without waiting for an answer, spilled hot oil on the beast's face. The eyes popped, flesh sloughed away and it fell to the deck. Gallagher stomped on it until it was little more than jelly and dust, just to make sure.

Another man—I'm fairly certain it was McGuinness the stoker—ran past us with one of the things clamped on his face. He went over the side without a sound and fell away. I ran to the rail to look over.

The sea below seethed, filled with the squirming, writhing tentacles of the beasts. I saw that three men had made a bolt for a rowboat, but they were caught and even now were little more than cold meat; food for scores more of the creatures that massed around the corpses, tentacles waving as if excited by the kill.

Almost as if the beasts knew I was watching, half a dozen heads turned, beady eyes staring up at me. A high wail, like a gull in the wind, came from six mouth parts, then as one they moved, scrambling up the hull, coming straight for me.

If *The Dubliner* had not lurched in a swell at that precise moment, I believe I would have been taken, for I was so transfixed at the sight of the creatures that I could not move from the spot. But when the deck tilted, Roberts too saw what was coming, and dragged me aside.

"To the stern, man," he shouted. "And pray the lifeboat is there."

We ran, even as the things clambered up over the gunwales and came after us.

Someone fell behind me, but I didn't even stop to look. Gallagher, Roberts and I were the only men still standing by the time we reached the stern. The sight that met us there made me fear that I was not going to outlive my old mates by very long.

A sperm whale lay on the platform—the whaler's last catch. And it was now obvious that the dead whale was also somehow the source of the infection. Its belly was vastly swollen and distended. I would have blamed a buildup of gases after its death, if I could not see the gaping hole in the blubber, and the writhing, seething nest of tentacled beasts all fighting to escape from within. It seemed the whale was little more than a carcass; a carcass filled to a bursting point.

It was equally obvious that our path to the stern lifeboat—if there even was a rowboat still there—was blocked by a slithering mass of the things.

"We can get to it from below, come up from under," Roberts said.

The thought of being trapped belowdecks with the creatures had me once again filled with dread, but I knew that Roberts was right. It might indeed be our only chance of escape.

But first, we had to find a safe place to get below, and that in itself was no easy matter.

The things were everywhere; they clambered over the bodies of our fallen mates, sucking and feeding in a most disgusting manner. The sounds and sights assaulted my ears and eyes such that I knew they would be repeated nightly in my dreams for evermore, even if I should survive this ordeal. The vessel rocked alarmingly beneath us, reminding us, as if we needed reminding, of the need for haste.

"We need to get off this boat," Gallagher shouted. Neither Roberts nor I disagreed with him. But the beasts blocked our way in every direction, and some were even now beginning to close in. I was considering a dive overboard—swim for it and hope for the best—when Roberts started to kick and stomp at any beast in range. They burst with moist squelches and lay still.

"The heads are their weak spot. We can make it," he said, pointing to his left at the hatch to belowdecks. "Just keep kicking."

We didn't need to be told twice. The three of us moved quickly across the deck in a series of stomping and dancing steps, leaving a trail of slime and mucus behind us. One of the beasts wrapped three tentacles around my ankle and squeezed, sending a flare of hot pain up the length of my leg. I brought my heel down hard and the head popped; the tentacles fell limply away. I dived through the hatch after Roberts.

Gallagher was just behind, and even as Roberts and I turned to pull the hatch closed, he fell through, screaming; one of the beasts had attached itself to his neck. The greedy mouth bored into the soft tissue between his neck and shoulder, and Gallagher's screams got louder.

But to the man's credit, he wasn't ready to lie down and die just yet. He yanked the thing away from him, tearing out a chunk of meat and skin of his own in the process, and threw it away. It hit the wall, fell to the floor with a wet thud, then started scurrying back toward us. Roberts stepped forward and brought his boot down on its head, twice, until finally it lay still.

We stood there, wide-eyed, staring at each other as we tried to remember to breathe. There was a single scream from above, quickly lost in the wind, then we heard the scurrying and slithering of the beasts moving overhead.

Suddenly all was silent save for the creaking of the old boat and the distant roar of the storm.

19

Present Day

I was brought awake with a start. Somebody screamed, and it took my befuddled brain several seconds to work out it wasn't a dream.

The scream came again, finally jolting me fully out of sleep. George seemed to be dancing around the room, in some strange parody of a waltz with a creature in his arms that I took for a dog at first before my eyes came into focus—then I realized what it must be. It was the thing from Pat's story—the thing from under the Village Inn porch—or something damned like it. A slimy body, with tentacles thrashing like snakes at George's belly even while he tried to keep a foul sucking mouth away from his face and a clacking, snapping pincer away from his hands.

Old Pat was about ten feet away, over by the coffee machine. He raised the kettle and threw it hard, but George had moved by the time it reached him and the kettle went straight for the wall—and straight through it, leaving a widening ripple where it had passed. Almost before the ripple had subsided, another of the creatures came through the wall, just where the kettle had vanished, and dropped on the floor with a moist thud before starting to scuttle in my direction. I felt the now-familiar warm tingle on the skin of my face and hands. The fog was nearby—and my guess was that these things were coming out of it.

We're in deep shit.

My first instinct was to help George, but before I got out of my seat, and he was gone—he stepped back, pushing the attacking creature away from his face, but stumbled and tripped. He fell toward the floor—and kept right on going, going through it like it was water. He didn't even get time to yell in alarm. The ripple he and the creature left behind hardened immediately, three waves in the hardwood boards that looked like they'd been there forever.

Old Pat and I looked at each other, dumbfounded, but there was no time to compare notes—the creature that had come through the wall was scurrying in our direction. Four eyes raised on thin stalks and swiveled until they looked straight at me.

"Out the back, lad," Pat shouted. "Quickly, now."

I didn't need a second telling, and although I had forty years on him, Pat beat me to it. He put his hand on the door and moved it slightly, but when he put pressure against it to force it fully open, his fist and forearm went right through. The wood hardened immediately, locking the old man into it as tight as a vise. He squealed in pain, all color draining from his face.

Something slithered at our back.

"I'm done for, boy." Pat said. "Save yourself."

I wouldn't be anyone worth saving if I left the old man to die. I turned back into the room, just as the tentacled thing made a lunge for my legs. I kicked out, hard, a lucky blow that caught it full in the body. It felt soft, like a deflated football, but it flew through the air well enough, hitting the stove with a dull thud and hissing where it touched the hot metal door. A rainbow shower of dust went up, then it lay still.

I headed for the panel in the wall and broke out the fire axe.

"Turn your head, old man. I'm going to get you out of there."

Pat's eyes were full of pain, and tears ran through the dust and grime on his cheeks, but he did as I asked and turned his head away from the door as I hacked with the axe.

I had to stop after the very first blow—it brought a scream of agony from the old man, the likes of which I never want to hear again.

"It's no use, boy—I'm a part of it now, and it's a part of me. Look."

I looked—although it was as hard to do it as it had been to look at Mrs. Malloy in her kitchen. Pat was right—they were part of each other. The wood of the door and the flesh of his arm had fused so that it was hard to tell where one ended and the other began. I was coming to think that if I hacked through the wood, I might find veins and muscle in there—and similarly, old Pat might have an arm of little more than pulp and wood fiber.

To my amazement, the old man managed a laugh.

"What are you going to do, boy—carry me and the bloody door around with you? You know what you have to do here. Get to it."

"I'm not leaving you," I said.

He grabbed me with his free hand.

"That's not what I'm asking, Frank. You know what you have to do."

His gaze fixed on the axe, and suddenly I knew what he meant.

I backed away, shaking my head.

"There's been enough dying for one night," I said. I was about to turn around when Pat's mouth fell open and his eyes went wide, looking past my left shoulder.

"Come here, Frank," Pat said through fresh tears. "Please—don't look round. Just come here."

Of course, I looked—anybody would. The far wall of the depot was shrouded in fog. I felt the warm tingle on my face again as the floor bucked beneath me. Indistinct shapes writhed and crawled just inside the fog—some had tentacles and claws—but others stood upright on two legs, although above the waist it seemed to me that their arms were too long—and too many.

"Leave, right now, Frank," Pat said. "Your father would have told you the same thing."

I moved to stand between the old man and the approaching fog, raising the axe in front of me.

"Don't do this for me, boy," Pat said at my back.

"I'm doing it for me, old man, now shut up, I'm busy."

My legs felt like jelly, and I could hardly hold the axe, but you know what? I felt more alive, more in control, than I had all night. This was something I could do, someone I could save. And I meant to spend my last breath doing it, if I had to.

It was as if my resolve gave the fog pause. It stopped advancing, and the obscured figures disappeared back into the murk as the fog swirled and thickened. It coalesced around a darker point at eye level straight ahead of me, a tear in space that glistened like black oil, rolling and turning and thickening into an egg-shaped droplet that hung in the air, quivering.

The walls of the depot throbbed like a heartbeat. The black egg pulsed in time. And now it was more than obvious—it was growing.

It calved, and calved again.

Four eggs hung in a tight group, pulsing in time with a throbbing vibration that was getting steadily louder and more insistent. Colors danced and flowed across the sheer black surfaces; blues and greens and shimmering silvers on the eggs.

In the blink of an eye, there were eight.

I was vaguely aware of Pat shouting at me, but I was past caring.

Sixteen now, all perfect, all dancing.

The vibration grew louder still.

Thirty-two now, and they had started to fill the depot with dancing aurora of shimmering lights that pulsed and capered in time with the throb of the vibration.

Sixty-four, each a shimmering pearl of black light.

The colors filled the room, spilled out over the floor, crept around my feet, danced in my eyes, in my head, all through my body. I gave myself to it, willingly. The depot filled with stars, and I danced among them.

I strained to turn my head toward the eggs.

A hundred and twenty-eight now, and already calving into two hundred and fifty-six.

A hand tugged at my shoulder and turned me round.

"Fight it, boy. If you don't fight it, nobody will," Pat said.

The depot was filling with what I guessed to be a thousand and twenty-four eggs.

"Fight it!" Pat shouted, and I remembered—Mrs. Malloy, and George, and the bus in the hollow and the Brodie house—all the terrors of the night fueling my anger. I hefted the axe and threw it, straight at the growing mass of black eggs.

Several things happened at once. The myriad of bubbles popped, burst and disappeared as if they had never been there at all. Pat screamed—a wail that was enough to set the walls throbbing and quaking. Swirling clouds seemed to come from nowhere to fill the room with darkness. Everything went black as a pit of hell, and a thunderous blast rocked the depot, driving me down into a place where I dreamed of empty spaces filled with oily, glistening bubbles. They popped and spawned yet more bubbles, then even more, until I swam in a swirling sea of colors.

I drifted.

When I got back—was given back—to what passes for reality, thin daylight lit the depot. There was no sign of the fog or the creatures it had brought with it.

Pat hung on the door, his hand still tightly embedded in the wood, his dead eyes staring up at me.

20

1856

From the journal of an unnamed seaman, discovered in Trinity town archives

At some point in the melee, I had quite lost my bearings. I thought we had descended to the area immediately above the engine room, but we were once again in the corridor that led to the crew quarters. And if the layout of the whaler was as I remembered it, there was no easy way to get to our objective in the stern from here.

"Our situation has hardly improved for the better," Gallagher said quietly. He bled heavily from the wound in his shoulder, but waved me away when I tried to help. "I'll have time for doctoring later, if we make it."

I looked to Roberts for guidance. He had bent to study the remains of the thing at our feet.

"What the hell are these things?" Gallagher asked. "I ain't never seen the like afore."

"Ain't never heard of the like either," Roberts replied, standing and wiping slime and mucus on his trousers. "It's some kind of squid, I think, but I'm buggered if I know anything more than that. Besides, what they are isn't important. We need to get to the stern, and fast. This boat is going into the rocks at any minute, and when that happens, we're all dead anyway."

I wasn't too keen on being reminded of that fact; I was still feeling happy at just having got below and away from the creatures. I looked down the corridor at the path we would have to take. Even with the presence of oil lamps at intervals, it was too dark to see more than ten yards or so, but my imagination filled in the blanks only too well. I started in that direction, but Roberts had other ideas.

"We could go farther down," he said. "The most direct route is through the main hold."

"But we have no idea what might be down there," Gallagher said.

"It can't be any worse that what's above us," Roberts replied. He lifted one of the few functioning oil lamps from its hook on the wall. "And the sooner its done, the quicker we can get off this death trap."

I followed him as he led us to the steps that led down into more darkness, hoping against hope that his last statement was close to the truth.

We found Irish Frank at the foot of the steps.

The creatures had got him—but not before he'd taken many of them with him. Charred remains lay strewn in a wide circle around the captain's body. A hole in his chest showed where he had finally succumbed. It hadn't been that long ago either, for the firebrand in his hand was still warm.

"He had the right idea," Roberts said, lifting the brand and getting it lit from the flame in the oil lamp. "We should have thought of it ourselves. See if you can find more of these. We might need them."

I found three long brands just by turning my head; I knew from experience that a supply was often kept near the entrance to the hold in whaling vessels. I passed one to Gallagher, and we lit up from the one in Roberts' hand.

Now we had enough light, we were able to see that we hadn't just found Irish Frank; we had found most of his crew. They'd tried to make a stand, here in the hold. It hadn't mattered; the creatures had found them and fed on them. They lay, piled on top of each other, or attempting to hide underneath barrels and crates or at the foot of another set of stairs where there had obviously been a fight among themselves in their rush to flee. And everywhere were the bloody trails that showed where the creatures had departed after feeding.

The boat lurched again, threatening to throw us off our feet. In a corner of the hold something scurried away.

We were not alone.

I expected Roberts to move, to head for the stern, but he and Gallagher had eyes only for the cargo. I saw that the hold was almost full; the whaler had made a profitable trip. The barrels sloshed as the boat rolled. They were full of oil.

"There's a king's ransom here," Gallagher whispered. "We've got to try to salvage what we can."

Roberts laughed bitterly.

"What we need to salvage is our lives."

Gallagher wasn't convinced, but he followed as we made our way quickly through the hold. There was no repetition of the scurrying sound, but I knew that I had heard it, and I jumped at every shadow, every creak of warping wood as we went forward.

When the attack came, it was from two directions. A fresh scurrying alerted me first. I turned toward it, just as the thing launched itself at me, tentacles reaching for my face. I got the brand between us, and hit the head square on. Something hissed, and the air filled with a stench that made me gag; hot spew filling my throat. I was aware of a commotion behind me; Gallagher and Roberts had troubles of their own, but I was too busy to pay attention to them.

The thing came at me again. I could just see that it was burned badly; one of the eyes had popped and dribbled noxious fluid on the deck even as it threw itself at me again. I poked it, twice, with the brand, and the flames took at the second attempt. The head went first. Tentacles writhed and thrashed in frenzy. It was only stilled when I brought my boot down, hard, squishing the burnt remains underfoot.

I turned back to my crew mates, looking for congratulation. There would be none forthcoming. They had not had my good fortune of hearing the attack coming. There was indeed a second burning beast on the deck at their feet, but it had done its own damage before succumbing. Roberts was still on his feet, but he was white as a sheet, apart from where a wash of blood ran down his chest, a gaping wound at his neck evidence of where the thing had penetrated his jugular.

"I'll be fine," he whispered, then his legs gave way despite Gallagher trying to hold him up. He fell at my feet; dead eyes stared up at me.

Gallagher took one look at the body, let out a wail, and headed forward at a flat run. There were more scurrying sounds in the darker shadows and, deciding discretion was the better part of valor, I too headed forward, as fast as I was able to while still ensuring I was safe from another attack.

I got to the stairs that led up to the stern just in time to see Gallagher step up onto deck some twelve feet above me. I flinched, expecting him to be immediately attacked, but all I heard was the whistle of the wind and the roar of water on rocks. The vessel struck something, hard enough to make me lose my footing and drop the brand. It hit the boards, snuffed out, and rolled away into darkness.

Something moved and skittered in the shadows.

I fled up the steps, expecting at any second to be hauled backward down into the dark. I was quite out of breath when I reached the deck.

Gallagher took no notice of me. He stood, staring, not toward the lifeboat at the stern, but forward. The lights of Trinity twinkled some quarter of a mile in the distance. By some miracle we had made it unscathed through the narrows and were even now being propelled ever closer to the main harbor.

"We can bring her in," Gallagher said. "Salvage the oil. We could be rich men by the morning."

I cannot say I wasn't tempted, if only for a second. Then I saw it in my mind's eye; the taverns and whorehouses overrun by tentacled beasts, burrowing into drunken flesh, feeding on babes and the old alike, taking the town by storm even before it knew what had happened. I knew in that instant I could never allow it.

But I could see by the look in Gallagher's face that he was lost in greed with no thought for the consequences. I did the only thing I could think of. I smacked him in the jaw, twice, as hard as I was able before he saw the punches coming. To my relief he fell, out cold. He was a big lad, but I was able to manhandle him onto the rowboat easily enough.

I left him there, took up his firebrand and, although every fiber of my being was telling me to flee, made my way back down into the hold to do what needed to be done.

It was dark down there. And once again every sound, every shadow, made me jump. But the fear of what might happen to my town was even stronger, and drove me forward. I kicked over the nearest barrel, then another, and two more before one finally obliged me and split open, spilling oil through the hold, a river running between the rest of the barrels.

The skittering sounds got louder, but did not approach any closer, and I actually managed a grim smile as I put brand to oil and the deck blazed in flame.

Once more I fled upward, fire nipping at my heels. A creature threw itself down at me from above but I was in no mood for pleasantries. I caught it by the tentacles, slung it around my head, and tossed it straight down into the flame. It took some layers of skin from my hand as it left, but that was a small price to pay to see it hit the fire and burst in flame.

The first barrel blew as I reached the main deck, the concussion almost blowing me off my feet. The whole vessel shook and lurched sharply to port. I had a bad couple of seconds when I couldn't find the winch for the lifeboat, and I only released it just as a second explosion almost tore the whaler in half. We fell, my stomach in my mouth, hitting the water hard and almost overturning before I was able to get an oar in my hand and start to put some distance between us and the now-burning whaler.

Gallagher woke, groggily, and had anger in his eyes as he saw what I had done. That anger quickly turned to terror as the sea between us and the rapidly sinking vessel started to seethe and roil. A mass of tentacles rose up, as if tasting the air, seeking us out. Scores of the creatures had escaped from the sinking ship…and they were making straight for us.

"Row, you bugger," I shouted, and Gallagher thankfully did not argue.

Two more explosions racked the stricken whaler, then a third, huge blast that filled the air with smoke and splinters and ash. When I could see clearly again, there was no sign that the boat had ever been there, save for a mass of wreckage bobbing on the waters.

But we were far from clear of danger. The tentacled beasts swam faster than we could row, and were now mere yards from overrunning us. I gripped the oar, meaning to use it as a club, ready to take some of them to hell with me.

And that's when the sound came from out beyond the narrows, a high wail, like the one we had heard from the creatures earlier, but deeper, resonant, like a great church organ being readied for play, high and clear even above the roar of the wind. The swimming beasts stopped in their tracks, their interest in us gone. Scores of mouths opened, the feeding tubes raised high out of the water. As one, they, too, wailed, answering some distant call. The noise from beyond the narrows grew louder, more insistent.

The swimming beasts started to move again, not toward us, but off toward the narrows.

I turned back to get our bearings, intending to head at all speed for the safety of the harbor, so I didn't see what Gallagher saw, but I recognized the shock in his face right enough.

"Oh my God, it's huge," he said.

He wouldn't speak of it again, not until later, in the warmth and comfort of the tavern.

"It filled the whole of the narrows," he said.

"What did?" I asked, but I was very much afraid that I did not want to hear the answer.

He replied in a whisper so none but I could hear, chilling me once more to the bone.

"The singing fog called them home."

21

Present Day

I staggered out of the depot into a snowy morning in Trinity—and that was all it was, just a bit of snow, large fluffy flakes drifting gently from a flat white sky. The wind had died almost completely. It looked like the storm had finally blown itself out.

But was there anything left to save?

Normally in the aftermath of a storm there would be sound—the scrape of shovel on ice, the whir and chug of diesel-powered snowblowers or the deep roar of the plows. This morning there was just silence, deep and ominous.

The snow was so deep I had to push and climb my way out of the depot parking lot and into the main road, which in itself was drifted higher than my head in places. I stood in the middle of the road and yelled at the top of my voice. The echo rang around Gun Hill behind the town, but that was the only answer I got.

I thought about getting the Skidoo running and doing another tour of the town—but that would mean climbing back over the drift around the depot, and I wasn't at all sure I had the energy for it. I made my way down the slope toward the church hall, slogging through drifts, almost rolling in places. There was no sign that anyone had been along apart from me. I felt like the last man alive.

That thought gave me pause.

What if I'm the only one left?

I found a crumpled pack of smokes in my pocket, and managed to get one straightened up and lit, the taste serving to remind me that I was running on fumes and in need of food—and coffee, lots of coffee.

I stood still for as long as it took me to finish the smoke, hoping to hear a sign of another living soul. The power lines hummed quietly overhead, but apart from that, there was only my own breathing and the thud of my heartbeat in my ears.

I flipped the butt away—the hiss it made as it hit the drift was the loudest noise around—and forced my way through the snowbank in search of company.

My first stop was at the church hall. It lay as empty as it had before, with no sign that anyone had been there since my last visit in the dark. The power was on though, and I was able to find the makings for a pot of coffee. Along with most of a packet of cookies, the brew did much to warm me up and make me feel a bit more human. I washed up after myself, more from a need to keep busy and stop myself from thinking than from any innate tidiness.

As I saw it, I had two options—make a run for it in the Skidoo, or use the same machine to do another tour of the town checking for survivors. I know what I wanted to do—but I also knew my duty. Too many had died on my watch already—there was only a life of booze and smokes ahead for me if I let them down again.

I left the hall, intending to make my way back up to the depot. That's when I heard it—I realized I'd been hearing it for a couple of seconds, it just hadn't registered. Somewhere close by a heavy engine—maybe more than one—was running.

And it was getting closer, fast.

The cavalry finally came over the crest of the hill above me.

There were three long silver trailer trucks, lined up behind the biggest plow I've ever seen. It cleared the church parking lot in only a few minutes, and seconds later the three trailers were lined up side by side on the gravel.

Everything was a frenzy of frantic activity for a while after that. The first two people I saw pointed guns at me, and the third shouted at me, so the cavalry weren't quite what I expected. They seemed more intent on setting up equipment than they were in either talking to me or searching the town, and when I tried to protest, I had a gun pointed at me again, so I decided to keep my peace for a while and observe.

They took over the church hall and within minutes had trestles, tables and chairs laden with high-tech laptops, oscilloscopes and a variety of pieces of hardware that I didn't understand. It was only when they had everything set up to their satisfaction that they deigned to talk to me, and by then I wasn't in the best of moods.

"What bloody kind of rescue is this?" I said as a tall, stocky man left one of the tables and came over to me.

He put out a hand for me to shake.

"Colonel Breem," he said. "I'm in charge here."

"I doubt that," I replied.

He smiled, but it didn't reach his eyes, and there was something about the way he carried himself that told me that maybe I shouldn't push too hard. But I was dog-tired, angry and ready to pop. So I pushed when I didn't get a reply to my first question.

"I said…"

"I heard you the first time," the man replied, and I got that smile again. "And I believe you've got the wrong end of the stick. This isn't a rescue. It's a research mission."

That took the wind out of my sails completely. I sat down and fumbled a smoke out of the packet. The man didn't join me.

He stood over me, and I was all too aware of his height and his bearing.

"We need to debrief you," he said. "We need to know what you've seen."

I stifled a laugh—once I started, I might not be able to stop.

"You came in past the campsite, didn't you? You saw what happened there?" The man nodded, but didn't speak. For the first time I saw what might be a spark of humanity in him, but he was keeping it down. I recognized the look. He had a job to do, and he meant to get it done.

"Is it the same all over?" he asked.

It was my turn to nod.

"Can you stop it?" I said.

He shook his head.

"We're not even sure what it is—that's why we're here. To get a handle on it, and try to figure it out. All we have is an old journal from the experiments in the fifties, and some heresay evidence from what might be some unreliable narrators. As I said—we need to know what you know. And we need to know it fast."

I told him what I knew. It took a while in the telling—he kept interrupting me to ask questions that I had no way of answering. Along the way I learned some of what they knew too, although it didn't help me much—talk of harmonic and magnetic resonance, plasma fields and parallel universes was the sort of stuff I normally switched off in favor of hockey when it turned up on the television.

After an hour he was frustrated, and so was I. We declared a mutual draw and decamped to the coffee-pot, at which point he lightened up—just enough that I noticed.

"At least the storm has passed," he said as he dropped three heaped spoonful's of sugar into his cup and stirred vigorously.

"Don't worry—there'll be another along soon enough. Welcome to *The Rock* in winter."

He waved a hand in the general direction of the door.

"The thing at the campsite—it's like that all over?"

I shook my head.

"As I said, we never got round to checking everybody—but that's what I'm worried about. If you would only..."

He put up a hand again.

"We've been over that already. My orders are to investigate and contain. And the investigation bit comes first. I'm not about to let my men go running about out there without protection."

"There is no protection from that thing."

That got me another grim smile.

"Maybe there is—the boffins have been working on something for years, and this is their chance to see if they've got it right. Come on—let me introduce you to the folks with the brains."

The brains were four people hunched over a table in the corner of the hall, and they were obviously far too busy to be interrupted just then. They seemed very excited about something on a large monitor.

"There it is," one of them said. "Just like we thought—a rolling ball of electromagnetic flux. This is awesome."

"*Awesome* isn't a word I normally use in the face of death and destruction," I said, suddenly angry again. All four turned to look at me as if I'd just arrived from another planet. "This thing has royally fucked my town—for all I know, everybody is dead. It's far from fucking awesome."

The original speaker at least had the good grace to look embarrassed, but all too quickly they were all crowded round the monitor again, babbling in incomprehensible—to me anyway—jargon.

"I need another smoke," I said, turning away.

Breem surprised me.

"I'll join you—let's stand by the door."

My remaining cigarettes were too bashed up, but he had a new packet that he opened with the practiced ease of a seasoned smoker. He passed me one, and lit us both with a flick of an old battered Zippo, the sound immediately reminding me of old Pat, who'd used one similar all the years I'd known him.

I looked out over my town—there was no smoke from any chimney, no sound but the hum of electrical equipment in the hall behind me. I was alone. And as quickly as that, I had tears running down my face, and a cold pit in my heart.

"What can I do to help?" I said.

Breem sucked smoke before replying.

"You've done a bit already—there's two places we need to see—both feature heavily in all the stories—the wreck site in Dunfield Bay…"

"Good luck with that," I replied. "The bay will be mostly iced over for weeks to come now after this storm. You won't get a boat out, and it's too treacherous to try walking over. But let me guess the other—I've heard the stories too—you'll want to see what's what in the Village Inn garden?"

Breem nodded.

"As soon as the brains are ready, that's our first stop."

"Then I'll take you there," I replied. "And we'll see whether they're as smart as they think they are."

It took a good quarter of an hour to get the plow and the three trailers down to the Village Inn and clear the small parking area enough for everything to fit in. It was a tight squeeze and the trailers and crew made enough noise to wake the whole town if anyone was listening.

Nobody came out to see what the commotion was about, and that in itself told me everything I needed to know—either survivors were too afraid to venture out, or the fog had got them all. Whether or not these new arrivals knew what they were doing, they were my only points of human contact—and I found that, this morning at least—I needed them.

I watched as they set up around the inn's garden. They had four tall stacks, each nearly six feet tall, almost like expensive audio speakers, placed in the corners of the space. Each of the stacks was then hooked by thick cabling to a heavy-duty generator in one of the trailers. When they switched it on, the air filled with a throb and hum that sounded far too loud in the quiet of the morning after the storm. It was still snowing, but when I looked up and saw that the flakes melted some three-feet above our heads, and no precipitation was reaching the ground.

Breem saw me looking.

"I told you," he said. "Containment. That's why we're here."

The four that Breem had called the brains went to sit inside one of the trailers—I caught a glimpse inside—more monitors, oscilloscopes and machines I couldn't fathom. I stayed out in the parking space, looking in to the garden with half a dozen armed men and Breem, all of us waiting, wondering what was coming next.

22

From the journal of Duncan Campbell, 25th July 1955

Muir had planned to wait for the light of day to make his attempt at healing both his body and the breach in reality we had caused, but over the course of the evening his state deteriorated markedly. By eight o' clock, I was starting to wonder whether he was even still human.

We had a light supper brought up to my room—if the innkeeper had seen what was sitting on the bed, we might have had to suffer far worse than being turfed out on our ears. Muir, as I have said, was going fast. Both his arms were now rather longer than they had been—almost serpentine and sinuous as they moved. His hands were still hands—but there was a definite web forming between each of his fingers, and Muir had been forced to remove his shoes as his feet had grown too long—stretched to almost comic proportions, and flattened—like flippers.

"For pity's sake, man, let's get you to a doctor," I said.

Muir laughed bitterly.

"And what do you think they'd do about this?" He lifted his shirt. Suckers covered his whole torso from neck to waist, moist red mouths gasping as if struggling for air. "And that's not the worst, Duncan."

"What in blazes could be worse?"

Muir tapped at his head.

"In here—I hear singing; I hear high, beautiful, singing. It's calling to me, constantly. I don't know how long I can hold out against it. I must go to that wreck again, Duncan. And it must be now—if we wait until morning, there might be nothing left of me and…"

He broke down and sobbed. I could have done something, I suppose—made some attempt at comfort. But I stayed in my chair, smoking a pipe and wondering whether it was too late to save myself.

I was so disgusted at having harbored the thought that when Muir announced it was now or never, I put on my outdoor clothes and accompanied him down to the jetty.

A welcoming committee waited for us, blocking our access to the boat. Our host, the innkeeper, seemed to be their leader, and it was he who spoke first.

"We can't let you go out to Dunfield, boys," he said. "You brought that mess to the shed the last time—we're not having any more of that nonsense."

"But this is important," Muir started. He was quickly interrupted; the innkeeper spoke again, his voice raised.

"You're not welcome here—how many times do you need to be told?"

I hadn't spotted it until now, but two of the men behind the innkeeper carried baseball bats, and another had a vicious-looking knife in his hand. I turned to Muir.

"Maybe discretion is the better part of valor," I said, but he brushed me off.

"I can't go backward, Duncan," he said softly. "It's too late for that."

He stepped forward, putting a foot on the jetty.

"That's far enough," the innkeeper said. The man stepped forward too, until the men were face to face.

"I don't want to hurt you, sir," the innkeeper said.

"I don't think you can anymore," Muir replied, and lifted up his shirt to let them all see the mass of gaping, wet-mouthed suckers.

They stood back in alarm.

"As you can see," Muir said calmly, still walking forward. "I have some kind of infection. And I am by no means sure of just how contagious it might be. I suggest you stand right back and let us get on with our business. Trust me, chaps—I want an end to it as much as you do."

Even then several of the men would not give way—that was until one of them looked down and got a good look at Muir's bare feet—after the rest of them noticed, they backed off pretty sharpish. I didn't blame them, for one look at those elongated flippers was enough to send my own mind into a spin, and I was rather glad when Muir stepped down into the boat and I could not see anything below his knees in the shadows.

I jumped in beside him. The local men glowered down from the jetty. They could have sunk us then if they'd thought of dumping some heavy stones on us, but they seemed transfixed by the sight of Muir, standing at the helm, shirt open to show the gasping suckers opening and closing in time with his breath.

Nobody spoke as Muir got the engine running and we pulled away from the jetty. I turned to look back as we crossed the bay—the dark figures were still there, silent, watching, as if meaning to ensure we would not return.

I was by no means sure of that outcome myself.

That trip in the dark will be forever etched in my memory. Muir was silent for the most part, but at least he had buttoned up his shirt, so I was spared the sight of the horrors being inflicted on his body.

There were other things, however, that could not so easily be hidden from sight.

My first hint that something was seriously amiss came at the mouth of the narrows even before we left the relative tranquility of Trinity harbor. The school of porpoises had beached on the shingle shore below the lighthouse—scores of them, piled one on top of the other as if they had fled the water in panic to throw themselves ashore. All were dead and already rotting although I had seen them swimming offshore mere hours before. The now-familiar dancing rainbow aura hung over the whole area, a shimmering light show of green and blue and gold. It was almost beautiful—and I could not bear to look at it.

Fixing my gaze straight ahead did not do much to ease my mind—Indian Head Rock seemed to shine out like a beacon in the night—brighter still than any lighthouse. As we got closer, I saw that it was lit as if in full daylight, despite the fact that we traveled under a moonless sky. Shadows flitted across the rock surface, clouds passing under a midday sun, an impossibility my mind struggled to comprehend. As we passed the rock, it threw reflected light over us, harsh shadows that seemed to caper and dance across our deck. I turned to Muir, meaning to ask what he made of it.

The sight that met my eyes caused me to fumble for a cigarette and once again turn my gaze forward—Muir stood at the helm—what remained of him. His eyes were opened wide, unnaturally large and almost bulbous, like those of a great fish. His mouth opened and closed as if gasping for air—and the gill slits in his neck pulsed in time. His shirt ruffled and squirmed where the suckers underneath seemed to quiver in frenzy.

I finally got my smoke lit and looked up at what lay ahead.

The whole surface of the sea between us and the Tern Rock that guarded Dunfield Bay danced in a rainbow shimmer, a shining path showing us the way forward. Despite Muir's greatly altered appearance, he apparently still maintained all of his faculties. He steered us straight and true along that path and brought us to a stop in the bay after taking lines of sight on several of the large rocks that jutted from the sea in these parts.

"We are here, Duncan," he said, his first words to me since leaving the jetty. There was a watery gurgle in his voice that I did not like to hear at all, but he seemed like his old self as he prepared the equipment, attaching cables, checking valves and making sure the batteries were ready to be attached. He even joined me for another smoke before we started.

"We shall make history tonight, Duncan," he said. "When I manage to control and then reverse the process, we will have finally uncovered the secret to manipulating the most basic nature of matter—we will bend creation to our will. Imagine it!"

I was indeed imagining it—although creation had, so far at least, shown a distinct unwillingness to be bent, and I was coming to think there might indeed be something in Muir's talk of a gatekeeper, some kind of police force of nature. I did not express my concerns to Muir—we were long past any point at which he might have listened to them. All I could do was observe, and hope to somehow get both of us out of there alive.

We finished our smokes in silence, then Muir pronounced that he was ready to start.

"Stay on the wheel, Duncan," he said to me. "If we drift, I need you to keep us above the wreck at all times—it is vitally important that the locus is under the field boundary—everything depends on that."

"And how exactly do I ensure such a thing?" I replied. "Drift is inevitable in this dim light."

Muir smiled—his teeth looked too white—and pointed. He motioned over the side of the boat.

"Light will be provided."

Something glowed down there—a diffuse gray that seemed to hang in the water at some depth beneath us.

"The way is open," Muir said. "Let us see where it takes us."

He attached the battery to his box of tricks.

It immediately started to hum.

23

Present Day

I felt the now-familiar tingle of static against my face as the hum in the inn's garden went up in volume. It throbbed and pulsed like some strange dance beat.

An excited cry came from inside the trailer.

"It's starting."

The garden went dark. I don't quite know how else to describe it—we stood in the dim glow of a morning under heavy snow clouds, but it was as if the garden itself had been plunged back under nightfall, so that all that could be seen inside was blackness and shadow.

That quickly changed when a blue light crackled, like a lightning strike, illuminating the same tumbledown shed I'd seen earlier, standing on clear ground without a hint of any snow. If it had been a vision then, it was one I was now sharing with everyone else, given the rapt attention that was being paid to it by all of us standing in the parking area.

"Increase the voltage," someone shouted inside the trailer. "There's too much fluctuation."

There was certainly too much of something. The air, even where we stood some yards back from the garden, cracked and crackled with static, and I felt the warm tingle on my face again.

"The fog's coming," I said, scarcely aware that I'd spoken out loud. I might even have turned and ran had Breem not put a hand on my shoulder.

"This is what we came for," he said. "We've got this under control."

A paler area appeared in the dark above the old shed, thin, like smoke at first, then thickening into the swirling, glowing fog that I'd hoped never to see again.

The humming went up a gear, vibrating in my jaw and gut. The fog drifted, leaving the spot above the shed and coming toward us.

"We need to get out of here," I said.

Breem shook his head.

"Wait and see."

The fog was only feet away now, and the tingling on my face and hands was like having electricity buzzing through me. The fog started to spark—blue and green and red, arcs of electricity running through the darkness. I ducked instinctively—but the fog didn't move any closer.

"Like I said," Breem said with a smile. "Containment."

24

From the journal of Duncan Campbell, 25th July 1955

"It's working," Muir said, although I was by no means certain of that.

Only minutes after switching his contraption on, fog started to rise from the sea all around us, glowing faintly and pulsing in time with the thrum and hum emanating from the kit on the deck.

I was more than aware that the deck, maybe even the whole craft, could go thin on us at any point, or that I could end up half-melted and trapped inside a fused piece of hull, but Muir showed no lack of confidence as he twisted the dials.

"I think I've got it," he said. "It's purely a matter of focusing the boundary—knocking on the door if you'd like to put it that way."

He turned a dial. The crystal valves flared, white, blue, then white again, so bright that I had to avert my gaze. The pale glow in the fog took on a blue tinge. Sparks flew, like arcs from a Van Der Graaf generator, making the hair on my arms stand on end. The sea around us started to bubble and seethe, so much so that I feared at first we were starting to boil—and my fear was not abated when I saw the real cause.

Thousands upon thousands of tentacled creatures no bigger than small dogs filled the water on all sides as far as I could see in the fog. They pressed tight against each other, squirming and rolling, tentacles gripping and coiling, suckers gaping—and small, vicious claws clacking with such a racket it quite overwhelmed the hum of the equipment on deck. Thousands of stalked eyes all looked in the same direction—toward the boat, but it seemed they were staring straight at me—I felt like I was being sized up for lunch. At least they showed no inclination to climb aboard the boat.

For now.

"If this is it working, I'd hate to see your idea of failure," I said.

Muir ignored me and fiddled with something in his box of tricks.

The fog immediately thickened and became almost palpable, a cold blanket wrapped tight around us. The creatures in the water fell still, although the eyes continued to swivel on their stalks, watching every movement we made. The air crackled with static, forked lightning in the fog before Muir seemed to calm matters with another calibration of the equipment.

"It's just like back in the shed," he said. "I think I have it now."

Even as he spoke, a black tear opened in the air above his head, accompanied by what sounded like the ripping of paper. A singe black egg, no bigger than my thumb, hung there.

"Well," Muir said. "We've had the door opened for us. Shall we step inside?"

Without waiting for an answer, he turned a knob. The egg quivered, a rainbow aura danced over it, and ever so slowly it became two, oily sheen running over their sleek black surface. They hummed to themselves, a high singing that was taken up and amplified by an answering whine from the crystal valves.

The creatures out on the water started to thrash and squirm in time to the beat.

As two eggs became four, the boat rocked from side to side in rhythm.

The dance had begun.

25

Present Day

Eight black eggs hung impossibly in the air above the old shed, oily and glistening, thrumming in time with the vibration that was getting ever louder, ever more insistent. I had to resist a sudden urge to start clapping in time to the beat.

Thick fog glowed and swirled angrily in the darkened garden, but whatever they were doing to contain it seemed to be holding, for now.

"What now?" I asked of Breem, who stood at my side. It seemed to take him some effort to drag his gaze away from the black eggs—sixteen now, and all dancing, all singing.

"All we can do is watch and learn," he said. "The brains are collecting data, but until we know more, we've got to let things take their course."

"And if the containment doesn't hold?"

The colonel smiled thinly.

"Then all bets are off. I'll race you to the mainland."

Seconds later, the sixteen became thirty-two, clustered in a tight ball that spun lazily in the air above the old shed. The structure itself was changing too—it had become noticeably thinner, almost translucent and swirling fog was clearly visible inside. It thinned further, almost a ghost now, then vanished completely until there was only the dark garden and the darker eggs hanging over it—sixty-four now, and singing louder.

The dust and ash in the blasted earth where the shed had been started to tremble and shake, then, as if taken by the wind, rose in a tight funnel spiraling up toward the hanging eggs, faster and faster still. The eggs sucked up the material and sang louder, as if requesting more.

I felt them suck at me too, and had the containment field not been in place, I think I might have been taken—and gone almost willingly—to whatever was on the other side.

There were too many eggs to count now—hundreds for sure. They almost filled the space in the garden, their song rising higher, the beat and thrum of the rhythm filling my head, and the dancing rainbow colors filling my eyes with blue and green and gold and wonderment.

26

From the journal of Duncan Campbell, 25th July 1955

The air above us was filled with singing black eggs, the sea was filled with thrashing creatures—and I was filled with the rhythm of the dance.

My whole body shook, vibrating with the rhythm. My head swam, and it seemed as if the hull of the boat melted and ran. The scene receded into a great distance until it was little more than a pinpoint in a blanket of darkness, and I was alone, in a cathedral of emptiness where nothing existed save the dark and the pounding chant.

And then there was light.

I saw stars—vast swathes of gold and blue and silver, all dancing in great purple and red clouds that spun webs of grandeur across unending vistas. Shapes moved in and among the nebulae; dark, wispy shadows casting a pallor over whole galaxies at a time, shadows that capered and whirled as the dance grew ever more frenetic. I was buffeted, as if by a strong, surging tide, but as the beat grew ever stronger, I cared little. I gave myself to it, lost in the dance, lost in the stars.

I don't know how long I wandered in the space between. I forgot myself, forgot Muir, dancing in the vastness where only rhythm mattered. I may even have been there yet had Muir not brought me back. He had me gripped by the shoulders and was screaming into my face.

"Duncan—fight it. Fight it, man. I need your help."

It was that simple request for humanity that brought me back—back from a place where humankind was as insignificant as one of the motes of dancing ash in the old shed. Although when I managed to focus on him, I could see that Muir was now as far gone from humanity as the stars among which I had been dancing. His head looked misshapen and deformed, as if his brain had grown too large for his skull and was threatening to expunge itself. His hands had taken on the same flipper-like aspect as his feet. The left one in particular bothered me—it had thickened and hardened into black cuticle. It looked like it wanted to become a claw. What is more, wet-mouthed suckers ran, not just over his torso but up and down both his arms.

"I don't have much time, Duncan," he said—even his voice was going, barely more than a throaty gurgle. "I need you to man the controls. Blasted fingers won't work anymore."

"I'll do what I can, old man—but I don't understand what you need."

He motioned me forward and pointed at a knob on the box of tricks.

"Turn that slowly clockwise when I tell you to," he said. "And follow my lead."

"Anything else?"

"Yes. Pray."

Muir went to stand at the prow and raised his hands until they seemed to be engulfed in the mass of the eggs.

"Now," he shouted.

I turned the knob.

The eggs danced faster—tens of thousands of them filling the sky above me with song and dance that I had to fight to resist. The sea boiled and seethed with trashing creatures. Muir sank his hands completely into the eggs.

"Turn it, Duncan. Turn it all the way."

I turned the knob to its full extent.

The myriad eggs popped, burst and disappeared as if they had never been there at all. Dancing fog swirled, a dark funnel overhead that brought a howling, screaming wind that threatened to overturn the boat.

Muir screamed.

Everything went black as a pit of hell, and a thunderous blast came down like a hammer from above, driving me down into a place where I dreamed of empty spaces filled with oily, glistening bubbles. They popped and spawned yet more bubbles, then even more, until I swam in a swirling sea of colors.

Lost.

27

Present Day

The end took us all by surprise.

The eggs—almost completely filling the garden now—pushed against the containment boundary, setting everything around us sparking with static, the vibration a deep bass drone that pounded in my gut and made me nauseous and dizzy.

Just as I thought I could take no more, there was sudden silence, a hiss and pop in my ears, as if the pressure had suddenly been taken off them. The eggs shivered, just once, then popped, releasing a rainbow burst of color that faded as the morning light washed away the darkness that had hung over the garden.

The containment field collapsed with a last fading wail, and we were left alone in the suddenly quiet garden, now knee-deep in snow again.

And that's when we saw we weren't quite alone. Something lay, squirming on the snow, right at the spot where the old shed would have been. Breem headed over toward it, motioning for me to follow.

Whatever was there, it was wailing pitifully, high-pitched and keening. I have never heard anything sound so lost.

As we closed in on it, I recognized the thing on the ground—it was another of those things from old Pat's story—the same as the one that had got poor old George in the depot. It was old Pat, George, and the fate of my town that I was thinking of when I brought my boot down, hard, in what passed for a face.

"Is it over?" I asked Breem.

He looked at the thing on the ground, then back at me.

"I have a journal I'm going to give you to read," he said. "And then perhaps you can tell me the answer to that question."

A rainbow shower of dust rose in the air from the thing at our feet, fell back to the snow, and was gone.

28

From the journal of Duncan Campbell, 25th July 1955

I woke in the dark, drifting and rocking on a quiet sea under a star-filled sky.

There was no sign of Muir, nor any of the eggs—the Keeper of the Gate had closed the way. When I looked overboard, I saw a dim light, fading out, far beneath us, sinking into the depths. Before I turned the craft back toward Trinity, I tipped Muir's kit overboard to send it down to join the rest of our failed experiment.

I got the engine going and left Dunfield Bay to seek out the nearest bottle of Scotch and get closely acquainted with it. I did not look back, and I shall never return.

I'm sorry to say that I cannot promise the same for the fog.

About the Author

William Meikle is a Scottish writer, now living in Canada, with over thirty novels published in the genre press and more than 300 short story credits in thirteen countries. He has books available from a variety of publishers including Dark Regions Press and Severed Press and his work has appeared in a large number of professional anthologies and magazines. He lives in Newfoundland with whales, bald eagles and icebergs for company. When he's not writing he drinks beer, plays guitar, and dreams of fortune and glory.

BIBLIOGRAPHY

NOVELS

The Green and The Black / Crossroad Press
The Boathouse / Crossroad Press
Ramskull / Crossroad Press
Songs of Dreaming Gods / Crossroad Press
The Dunfield Terror / Crossroad Press
Fungoid / Crossroad Press
The Hole / Crossroad Press
The Exiled / Crossroad Press
Night of the Wendigo / Crossroad Press
The Ravine / Dark Regions Press
The Invasion / Dark Regions Press
The Valley / Dark Regions Press
The Creeping Kelp / Dark Regions Press
Crustaceans / Dark Regions Press
Sherlock Holmes: The Dreaming Man / Gryphonwood Press
Berserker / Gryphonwood Press
The Midnight Eye Files: The Amulet / Gryphonwood Press
The Midnight Eye Files: The Sirens / Gryphonwood Press

The Midnight Eye Files: The Skin Game / Gryphonwood Press
The Concordances of the Red Serpent / Gryphonwood Press
Watchers: The Coming of the King / Gryphonwood Press
Watchers: The Battle for the Throne / Gryphonwood Press
Watchers: Culloden / Gryphonwood Press
Watchers: Omnibus edition / Gryphonwood Press
Eldren: The Book of the Dark / Gryphonwood Press
Island Life / Gryphonwood Press
The Road Hole Bunker Mystery - Charade Media

NOVELLAS

Operation: North Pole / Severed Press
Operation: Orkney / Severed Press
Operation: Patagonia / Severed Press
Operation: London / Severed Press
Operation: Sahara / Severed Press
Operation: Yukon / Severed Press
Operation: North Sea / Severed Press
Operation: Congo / Severed Press
Operation: Mongolia / Severed Press
Operation: Norway / Severed Press
Operation: Syria / Severed Press
Operation: Loch Ness / Severed Press
Operation: Amazon / Severed Press
Operation: Siberia/ Severed Press
Operation: Antarctica / Severed Press
Infestation / Severed Press
The Lost Valley / Severed Press
Sea Hunters: Shonisaurus / Severed Press
The Land Below / Severed Press
The Sea Below / Severed Press
The City Below / Severed Press
Tormentor / Crossroad Press
Clockwork Dolls / Crossroad Press

Sigils and Totems: A Collection of Novellas / Crossroad Press
Broken Sigil / Crossroad Press
Pentacle / Crossroad Press
The Job / Crossroad Press
The House on the Moor / Dark Regions Press
The Plasm / Dark Regions Press
Professor Challenger: The Island of Terror / Dark Regions Press
Sherlock Holmes: Revenant / Dark Regions Press

SHORT STORY COLLECTIONS

Inspector Lestrade: The Black Temple / Weird House Press
The Ghost Club / Crystal Lake Publishing
Dark Melodies / Dark Regions Press
Carnacki: Heaven and Hell / Dark Regions Press
Carnacki: The Watcher at the Gate / Dark Regions Press
Carnacki: The Edinburgh Townhouse / Lovecraft ezine
Carnacki: Starry Wisdom / Dark Regions Press
Sherlock Holmes: The Quality of Mercy / Dark Regions Press
Professor Challenger: The Kew Growths / Dark Regions Press
The Midnight Eye Files: Omnibus / Gryphonwood Press
The Midnight Eye Files: Omnibus 2 / Gryphonwood Press
Samurai and Other Stories / Crystal Lake Publishing
Myth and Monsters / KnightWatch Press

Printed in Great Britain
by Amazon

60890695R00119